"Whoa, there," Cad

His lips brushed he ___ much faster than when she was falling. "I—I think so."

Yet she clung to him, closing her eyes, relishing the security, being in his arms.

"Dawn."

She was well aware that she was plastered up against his body, chest to chest, hips to hips, thighs to thighs. "Hold me, just a little longer, Cade."

He tightened his grip on her and she relaxed against him. She didn't want to think about the ramifications of this little slipup.

And so when Cade put a finger under her chin and she lifted her eyes to his, she found hunger and want. "Cade," she whispered.

"I'm gonna kiss you, Dawn. Fair warning."

And when she didn't protest, didn't back away, tenderly he cupped the sides of her face and brought his mouth down on hers.

* * *

Craving a Real Texan by Charlene Sands is part of The Texas Tremaines series.

Dear Reader,

I will admit, I'm not a huge fan of reality television, although I enjoy talent and cooking shows. I do find dating shows fascinating, and as I was plotting this first Tremaine story, ideas ran wild in my head of a heroine who is on her way professionally as a talented chef. All that is missing in her life is true love. She's failed at achieving that in the conventional way, so she is coaxed into going on the reality show *One Last Date*. We meet Harper Dawn after she goes from being America's darling to becoming one of the most hated women in the country when she declines an offer of marriage from a beloved contestant on national TV.

I love a woman-on-the run story, don't you? Harper runs from the paparazzi hounding her and finds solace at her dear friend's remote lake cabin only to find she is not alone. Rich and gorgeous Cade Tremaine has his own valid reasons for being at the cabin. He's a man running from his past, a man who'd been ordered by his doctor to take a much-needed vacation.

The fun begins when Harper pretends to be Cade's personal chef. Cade has no idea who Harper really is. He thinks reality shows are ridiculous—how can you find love in only a few short weeks? Yet, sharing a cabin with the pretty and talented Harper might just change his mind.

I hope you enjoy visiting the Tremaine family. I'm hard at work now writing Gage's love story. And who knows, maybe even sister Lily will find love, too!

Happy reading!

Charlene

CHARLENE SANDS

CRAVING A REAL TEXAN

HARLEQUIN
DESIRE

HARLEQUIN®
DESIRE™

ISBN-13: 978-1-335-23277-9

Craving a Real Texan

Copyright © 2021 by Charlene Swink

This edition published by arrangement with Harlequin Books S.A.

For questions and comments about the quality of this book, please contact us at CustomerService@Harlequin.com.

Harlequin Enterprises ULC
22 Adelaide St. West, 40th Floor
Toronto, Ontario M5H 4E3, Canada
www.Harlequin.com

Printed in U.S.A.

Charlene Sands is a *USA TODAY* bestselling author of contemporary romance and stories set in the American West. She's been honored with the National Readers' Choice Award, the CataRomance Reviewers' Choice Award and is a double recipient of the Booksellers' Best Award. Her 2014 Harlequin Desire title was named the Best Desire of the Year.

Charlene knows a little something about romance—she married her high school sweetheart! And her perfect day includes reading, drinking mocha cappuccinos, watching Hallmark movies and riding bikes with her hubby. She has two adult children and four sweet young princesses, who make her smile every day. Visit her at www.charlenesands.com to keep up with her new releases and fun contests. Find her on Facebook, Instagram and Twitter, too: Facebook.com/charlenesandsbooks and Twitter.com/charlenesands.

Books by Charlene Sands

Harlequin Desire

The Texas Tremaines

Craving a Real Texan

The Slades of Sunset Ranch

Sunset Surrender
Sunset Seduction
The Secret Heir of Sunset Ranch
Redeeming the CEO Cowboy

Visit her Author Profile page at Harlequin.com, or charlenesands.com, for more titles.

You can also find Charlene Sands on Facebook, along with other Harlequin Desire authors, at Facebook.com/harlequindesireauthors.

To Don, my loving husband and lifelong best friend. Always.

One

"I'm here now, Lily," Harper Dawn whispered into the cell phone. "I don't think anyone saw me."

At least she hoped not. She'd emptied a box of dark chestnut-brown color onto her hair, changing her look from a soft honey blond to shiny brunette in a matter of minutes. She'd cut her signature waist-length locks to fall just below her shoulders now, and the transformation surprised even her. Hopefully her disguise was enough to fool the paparazzi.

"How did you manage it?" Lily asked. Her friend sounded relieved. No more than she was. Right now, she was probably the most hated reality star on the planet for dumping her seemingly perfect guy, a chef like herself, in front of millions who'd followed their love affair on national TV. "How'd you get out of your apartment complex without being seen?"

"It was tricky. My neighbor Tony walked me out. I'm in disguise now. You won't even know it's me." She spotted Lily's car passing her on the street. "In fact, you just drove by me."

"What? I didn't see...oh, wow. Okay, I see you now on the library steps. Hold on, I'm turning the car around."

Harper laughed for the first time in three days, ever since her big breakup on *One Last Date*, and the sound was welcome to her ears. If she could fool her onetime college roomie, then this little plan Lily had cooked up might just work.

Her friend stopped the car, and Harper quickly jumped in. It was like a movie scene where Harper was the bank robber and Lily drove the getaway car. "Wow," her friend said. "You do look different. How are you holding up?"

"Better, now that I'm with you."

Lily punched the gas pedal, and they were off. "I'm glad you got away. Do me a favor and don't look at your Twitter feed anytime soon."

"That bad?"

Lily nodded. "Worse, and I can't help but feel responsible for this. I suggested you go on the show. But honestly, Harper, I had no idea it could all go to crapola so quickly."

"It's not your fault. You didn't twist my arm. Too much." Harper gave her a crooked smile. "I don't blame you. I should've known better."

"You're looking for love. Everyone should have a chance at happiness, Harp. Including you."

"I'm beginning to think I won't ever find it. Let's face it—I'm thirty years old and have had one broken relationship after another. Either I'm a bad judge of character or I'm totally unlovable."

"BS, Harper," Lily said, taking her eyes off the road to shoot her a solemn look. "You are neither of those things. You just haven't met the right guy. When you do, it'll be like creating the perfect soufflé. You'll get all gooey inside."

Harper laughed for the second time in less than an hour. "You're using foodie examples to persuade me."

"Is it working?"

"Not at the moment, but keep trying and eventually it will."

"Good. Well, here we are. This is where I leave you." Lily parked beside a white sedan in the Good Times Diner lot and handed her the keys to the rental car.

"Whose car is this?" Harper asked.

"It's a rental. In my name, so no one will be able to find you. Hopefully. Oh, and here," she said, handing her a big duffel bag. "You'll need some clothes and things. I put a spare computer in there, too."

"Lily, this is so…sweet. You've thought of everything. I promise, I'll repay you for all of this."

"Don't worry about it. Your birthday's coming up. Consider it your gift."

"My birthday? That's not for two months."

"Well, I didn't think you'd get away with walking out of your apartment complex with any luggage."

She sighed. Lily was the best friend she'd ever had. "You drove all the way from Juliet County to come rescue me."

It was an hour drive from the Tremaine estate in Juliet County to her little town of Barrel Falls. She'd only lived here a few months before she'd gotten picked for the show. And she'd put her professional life on hold to find love. Now, Lily was giving her an opportunity to escape the media that had followed her here from Los Angeles.

"No thanks necessary. Just go up to the cabin and try to relax. There's plenty of room there. You can work on your cookbook and no one will bother you. I wrote down the address. It's up in the hills and quite beautiful. Use the GPS to find your way. You've got a good two-hour drive, so be careful on the road. And we'll talk often, I promise."

"Okay," Harper said, nodding and taking a steadying breath. "Nothing like this has ever happened to me before. I feel like I've committed a crime or something."

"Harper, you followed your heart. You didn't love Dale Murphy, and you did the right thing by breaking it off. I guarantee you in a week or two, this crazy fiasco will be over and you can come home to peace and quiet."

"This is…" Harper bit down on her lower lip as tears welled in her eyes. "You're such a good friend, Lil."

Lily was the only daughter in the Tremaine family, one of the richest families in Juliet County if not in all of Texas. She and Lily had been college roomies at Stanford and vowed to remain friends for life. Both had decided on different career paths, Lily going into interior design and Harper opting for culinary school. "You'd do the same for me, Harper. I know that for sure."

Harper climbed out of Lily's car and hopped into the rental car. She waved at her dear friend.

Then she was off, driving to a remote cabin up in the Texas hills.

Take a vacation, Cade. You're working yourself too hard.

Dr. Adams had laid down the law after a physical exam had confirmed high blood pressure—way too high for a man in his early thirties. Cade had insomnia most of the time and walked the halls at night, too keyed up to sleep. He'd been pouring himself into the family business, putting in too many hours at Tremaine Corp., and his body couldn't handle the strain much longer. So said the doc.

Cade Tremaine sat down on his bed, rubbing his forehead. He'd been an athlete in high school and college, playing baseball while earning degrees in business and communications. He'd prided himself on good health and keeping his body fit. But that was before he'd lost Bree, the love of his life and the world's most perfect woman, to a cruel disease a year and a half ago.

Now, he shuddered at the idea of being alone with his thoughts, of not working, not pushing himself to the brink to keep his mind occupied and his grief at bay. Running the Tremaine ranch, keeping their oil business and real estate interests right on track was his whole life now. But the doctor had told him quite forcefully he had to take a break. Either that or go on a slew of medications to combat his physical problems.

This was the one time that he wished he was more like his brother Gage. The outgoing country music star never seemed to get rattled. He was as cool as a cucumber and let things slide off his back, whereas Cade bottled things up inside. Cade, the oldest of two brothers and one sister, had helped pick up the pieces when his father, Brand, had passed away eight years ago. And since then, Cade had done everything he could to keep the business and the family thriving.

His mother entered his bedroom. Head held high, she had stately elegance and commanded attention whenever she walked into a room. Rose Tremaine treated everyone equally, from the housekeeper to the mayor of Juliet, setting a good example for her family. They'd often teased that she was really Helen Mirren disguised as their mother.

"Cade, I see you're all packed up."

"Yeah, Mom. I'm packed."

"I'm glad you're going up to the cabin. It'll do you good."

"Will it, Mom? I don't know."

"You need a change of pace, Cade. And work can

wait. We have Albert at the helm at Tremaine in your absence, and he's capable."

"We have that possible merger I've been busting my butt on."

"Cade," his mother said, "are you forgetting who helped start this company with your father? I'm here, and Albert knows he can look to me if he needs any help. But son, this is a good thing. You haven't really come to terms with Bree's death."

"How can you say that, when it's with me all the time?"

"That's exactly my point. This is a good opportunity for you to shed some of that grief you've been holding inside. You've gone on a downward spiral lately. You don't eat well, you hardly sleep. You work yourself into the ground. None of that's healthy."

"You sound like my doctor," he grumbled. He wasn't thrilled about any of this. He squeezed his eyes closed. He hated the notion of being alone at the cabin with his mental demons.

His mother kissed his cheek and patted his face. "I'm your mother, and Mother knows best. I promise this trip will do you good. I've called ahead, and everything is ready for you."

"Thanks, Mom."

His mother sure knew how to get things done.

Then his thoughts turned to Bree. Holding on to his grief meant keeping her close in his heart. Somehow, it felt like he was betraying her by trying to move on with his life.

He wasn't sure he was ready to let go.

* * *

What a difference a day or two made. Harper couldn't believe less than a week ago, she was being hounded by the media, running away from paparazzi and being touted as the most hated woman in all of TV land. Oh no, she hadn't taken Lily's advice as she should have. Instead, curiosity had gotten the best of her and she'd ventured into the Twitter-sphere, coming out scarred and shaken. Not that she didn't have some support on social media. There were a few brave souls who'd taken her side, more rational human beings who hadn't fallen for Dale Murphy's charm and wit, finding instead that he and Harper weren't a good match.

But today was a different story. She hummed along with the radio playing Gage Tremaine's latest country hit—the story of a man falling on hard times and coming out a winner because of the love of a good woman. To this day, she could hardly believe that gorgeous Gage Tremaine, famous country music star, was Lily's brother. She'd never met either of her friend's two brothers, their paths never crossing, but Lily spoke of them often while they were roomies. In a loving way, *mostly*. And now, here Harper was, staying in the Tremaine cabin, which was more like a four-bedroom estate overlooking a lake in a glorious and remote mountain community, cooking herb-roasted chicken in their state-of-the-art kitchen. The luscious scents of sage, rosemary and garlic filled the air, almost bringing tears of joy to her eyes.

This place was amazing. Peaceful. And paparazzi-free.

She pulled the roaster out of the oven and covered

it with foil. The only thing missing was a kale salad. The fridge had been stocked when she'd gotten here, except for fresh fruits and veggies. Today, she'd venture out for the first time in two days to do some shopping. If Lily was right, hopefully by now the hoopla about her breakup with Dale was yesterday's news.

She put on a ball cap and tossed on her hoodie. Though the spring air was warm, the hills this time of late afternoon could get cold. She slipped on a pair of sunglasses and ventured outside. The market in Bright Landing was a short mile and a half away. She left her rental car behind and headed out on foot, enjoying the fresh mountain air.

Before long she'd reached her destination and entered the quaint but well-stocked Bright Market. She grabbed a basket and walked down the aisles, finding ingredients she needed for her salad: kale, broccoli, green cabbage, Brussels sprouts and radicchio. Her basket was brimming to the top with fruit and veggies by the time she was through.

She turned the corner of the aisle and bumped right smack into a man. A tall man, with dark hair and a chest hard as granite. "Oh, sorry. I didn't see you," she said, catching her balance, feeling grossly inelegant as an apple spilled out of her basket.

"I didn't see you, either." His voice was rich with a Texas twang, and his words made her feel like less of a clod. "Are you okay?"

"Yes, I'm fine."

He noticed the fallen apple and bent to pick it up, dropping it into her hand. Their eyes met. She blinked, reeling from the immediate impact of his dark, soulful gaze. She saw something in his eyes, something akin to well-hidden pain. And it touched her, making her wonder what had happened in his life to elicit such a look.

She realized she was staring at him, and he was staring right back. He smiled, in stunning contrast to the pain she'd witnessed in his expression just a second ago. *Wow.* His smile made something click inside and go a little wacky.

But then, out of the corner of her eye, she spotted a tabloid newspaper sitting on a rack at the checkout counter with a photo of her as a blonde splashed across the front page. The headline read, Where Is Heartbreaker Harper? Chef Dale Murphy Wants to Know.

Oh man. It was proof positive the scandal hadn't gone away. No, it was still going strong if it had reached the outskirts of a small hillside town like this. Warning bells went off. Her heart began to pound. She wasn't safe anywhere. Luckily, her disguise was holding up, because customers in the store were walking by her, and the handsome man she'd bumped into hadn't shown any recognition.

Thank goodness. "Excuse me," she said to him as she made a beeline to the checkout stand. She kept her head down and paid for her groceries. Once she was out of the store, she sighed in relief.

But that small triumph didn't keep her from trembling down to her toes, from feeling totally exposed and vulnerable again. The things they were writing about her weren't true. She wasn't a heartbreaker, or fickle or cruel. She hadn't played games with Dale's heart. She hadn't meant to hurt anybody. All she'd wanted was to find love, the long-lasting kind, and share a life with someone she felt connected to. The entire world seemed to think Dale being a chef like her meant they were perfect for each other, and for a time, she'd believed it, too. But it seemed the only real flames they'd sparked were at the kitchen stovetop. And her only real crime was that she'd found out too late she really admired Dale, the chef, but she didn't like Dale, the person, all that much.

She rushed back to the cabin in half the time it had taken to get to the store and put her groceries away. Her hands still shaking, she donned her pink-and-white polka dot apron and began putting together a salad. Cooking always relaxed her. It was the balm she needed now after seeing that tabloid. She ripped the kale and tossed it in a bowl, then chopped fresh broccoli and slivered cabbage strips. Calmer now, she began humming, grateful to Lily for giving her this chance to hide out and clear her head. Her cell phone rang, and she nearly jumped out of her skin.

Which wasn't good when you were holding a knife. A quick glance at her cell confirmed it was her friend calling. *Thank goodness*. "Lily, hi."

"Hi, Harper. How's it going?"

"It's going. I've settled in and love the place. But I just saw a photo of myself on the front page of a tabloid at the tiny market here, so I guess the story is still going strong."

"Sorry, Harp. Give it some time. It should get better."

"I hope you're right. It's hard to see that right now. And you, my friend, didn't tell me that this *cabin* is more like a dream home. I mean it, Lily. The place is beautiful. Thank you, a thousand times thank you for letting me stay here. It's so generous of you and your family."

"Well, uh, about that. I do have one teeny, tiny favor to ask you." Lily's voice went up two octaves, almost to a squeak.

"Anything. You know I'll do anything for you."

"Okay, well. You might change your mind when you hear what it is."

"I'm listening, Lil."

"My big brother, Cade, is on his way up to the cabin, too. Sorry, but my mother and I didn't coordinate on this, and honestly, sometimes a whole year goes by before anyone uses the place. But the truth is, ever since his fiancée passed away, Cade's been working himself to death. You've never gotten the chance to meet him but he's a really good guy and he's never given himself time to get over his loss. Now his blood pressure is way up. He's not eating right, either, and his doctor has warned him to slow down and take better care of himself. He ordered him to take a vacation. Which Cade didn't want to do. At all. My mom had to use clever tactics to get him to agree to leave work."

"Oh dear. I'm sorry to hear that. I guess," she said,

nibbling on her lip, feeling a crushing blow coming her way, "I'd better leave."

"Don't be silly. You have nowhere else to go. I know that and you know that. Your disguise is working, but maybe only because you're in a small town and not under intense scrutiny. You can stay. It's a big place."

"But—"

"If we tell Cade the truth, he'd insist on leaving and letting you have the cabin. He doesn't want to be there, and this would only give him an excuse to go back to work. Which he cannot do. He needs to relax."

"So, what are you saying?"

"Well." Lily's voice lowered. "I've already cleared this with my mother. She's adamant that he stay. So what if we say my mother hired you to be his personal chef?"

"What?"

"You are a chef, Harper. And he hasn't been eating right. It's not out of the norm for my mother to do something like this."

"You want me to pretend I was hired by your mother?"

"Yes, but you'd have to use a different name. Even though you haven't met him, he's heard me talk about my friend Harper. He'd never recognize you from the show. The man never turns on the TV. Other than sports, that is. He wouldn't be caught dead watching a reality show. It could work. And it's only for a week or two."

"But—"

She heard a car pull up into the driveway, fallen leaves crunching under the tires. *Oh no.* Her pulse raced. She had little time to think. "He's here."

"What are you going to do?" Lily whispered in a rush.

What could she do? Lily was a dear friend. She'd put herself out to help her, and Lily's brother's health was at stake. It didn't seem as if she had a choice. "I'll do it," she said. "I'll tell him Rose hired me to cook for him."

"Oh, wow. That's a relief. Thank you, Harper. We'll talk soon and—"

"Gotta go. I hear him at the door."

"Okay, good luck."

She ended the call just as a key was turning in the lock at the front door. She stood there, waiting, holding her breath. And the irony hit her smack upside the head. She'd gone from one crazy scenario on a reality show to another nutty scheme within a blink of the eye. Oh boy, what happened to the quiet girl who'd loved to stay home at night testing recipes, happy to have the role as head chef in her hometown restaurant? Where had that girl gone?

She stared at the front door, making no attempt to go and open it. A tan duffel bag was tossed through first, landing inside the foyer. And then the man followed, carrying a piece of black luggage.

Her heart pounded as he made his way over the threshold. "You," she said almost inaudibly. It was the man from the market.

He startled and shook his head as if seeing things.

Had she scared him? Immediately, their eyes met. Oh wow, those dark eyes again. They touched her in ways she couldn't name.

"You're the girl from the market."

She nodded and wiped her hands on her apron. "I am."

"What are you doing here?" he asked, setting down his luggage. He kept a safe distance from her, an honorable act on his part. He seemed sensitive to her possible fear. Then he noticed her apron and lifted his nose in the air. The scent of rosemary-herb chicken wafted up. "Something smells awfully good."

"Thank you." She smiled. "I'm Dawn." As in Harper Dawn. Okay, so she wasn't quick on her feet, but her last name made a good enough first name in this situation. "And I'm your personal chef."

Cade stared at the woman he'd bumped into thirty minutes ago. She was standing in the kitchen doorway looking at him warily, as if she feared he'd bite her head off. That she was his personal chef gave him pause. "Funny, I don't remember hiring a personal chef."

"You didn't. Your mother, Rose, hired me."

On a sigh, Cade rubbed the back of his neck. He didn't doubt the woman. It made damn near perfect sense. His mother was a woman of action and wasn't one to take no for an answer. If she'd asked him about it, he would've told her he didn't need a chef. But honestly, deep down, the thought of having someone else around, especially a cook, meant he didn't have to be totally alone. With his memories. With his grief. With his shattered heart. "That sounds like my mother. She knows I can't cook a lick."

"Not a lick?" she asked.

"I can boil an egg. Period."

"Well, that's a start."

Where were his manners? "I'm Cade," he said, putting out his hand. "Nice to meet you, Dawn."

She hesitated a second, then shook it and smiled. A pair of delicate dimples appeared. Bree had had dimples, too, but with that, the similarities ended. Bree had been a lush redhead, with incredible green eyes and soft porcelain skin. This woman's eyes were intense blue, her skin a creamy tan, as if she'd spent a lot of time outdoors, and her hair shone in the cabin light, a rich chestnut brown.

He shouldn't be comparing the two women, but he found himself comparing women to Bree all the time. And the other women were always coming up short. It wasn't fair of him. He was better than that. Yet he couldn't seem to help it.

"I guess I'll get settled in, then," he said. It was awkward, having a young woman living in the cabin. "Do you live nearby?"

"No. Actually, I live in Barrel Falls, about eighty miles from here."

"That's not far from Juliet County. We're practically neighbors. So then, you'll be staying here, too?"

"Yes, but I promise not to get in your way. I'm... working on a cookbook. So I'll be testing out recipes and logging my results most of the time."

His brows furrowed. "A cookbook, huh?"

"A dream of mine. But don't let me keep you from getting settled. I took one of the downstairs bedrooms, if that's okay. Unless you want it?"

"No, no. I'll be fine upstairs." All four of the bedrooms were master suites, two up and two down, and each one had all the luxuries a person could ask for. He'd never brought Bree to Bright Landing, so at least he had no memories of her here.

Dawn pointed to the kitchen. "I've got a roast chicken keeping warm, and I'm just finishing up on a salad, if you're hungry."

"If it tastes as good as it smells, I'll be right down."

"Okay then." She fidgeted with her apron. "See you in a bit."

He nodded and then climbed the stairs, picking the blue room. It was his favorite, with a killer view of the lake against the backdrop of oak trees and verdant hills. He set his suitcase down and went into the bathroom to wash up. He turned on the faucet and yelped as he splashed the icy-cold water on his face. Then he chuckled, remembering that it took forever to get hot water up to the second floor. He was ten when his folks bought the cabin, and he and his brother, Gage—and Lily, too—would fight over who'd get the downstairs rooms for that very reason. In this case, the cook—or rather, his personal chef—had the honors. But now that he was older, he didn't mind waiting for warm water if it meant waking up to the hillside panorama.

Cade was dressed in a fresh change of clothes

within ten minutes. He combed his dark straight hair back, noting that the thick mop was in need of a cut. He hadn't thought he'd have to worry about his attire up at the cabin, but now that Chef Dawn was here, he'd need to take better care of his appearance. He hadn't brought much in the way of clothes, just jeans, T-shirts and a few sweaters. He wasn't planning on being here all that long. Ten days at most. With nothing to do.

"Man," he muttered, glancing at himself in the mirror and seeing a forlorn face staring back at him. "This isn't going to be fun."

He opened his luggage and pulled out a framed photo of Bree and him when they were at their happiest. He had his arm around her, and they were smiling into the camera, love shining in their eyes as they stood on stage right before one of Gage's concerts. They'd been in Austin at the time, and they'd gotten the VIP treatment. Bree had been fascinated and thrilled, but instead of going gaga over his superstar brother, as so many of his dates had, Bree focused all of her attention on Cade, giving him sweet smiles and loving kisses. It was the night he realized how much he loved her.

"This isn't moving on, is it, Bree?" He smiled sadly and set the photo back in his suitcase, then made his way downstairs.

"Are you a kitchen eater? Or do you prefer the dining room?" Chef Dawn asked as he entered the room. She held a plate in her hand, ready to dish up the food. The kitchen was spacious, and the light oak table was big enough for ten. The dining area was used only for holidays and special occasions.

"Kitchen is fine. Unless I'll be in your way."

"Not at all."

She set his plate on the counter and dished up the food: roasted chicken and fingerling potatoes with a mixture of herbs that made his mouth water. She drizzled a bit of extra virgin olive oil over the entire meal and then pointed to his place at the head of the table and set the dish down. A salad bowl was already on the table, next to a vase of colorful wildflowers. It was a nice touch.

"What would you like to drink?" she asked.

"Let me see what we have." He opened the double-door fridge and found everything neatly in place: drinks to one side, dairy products on the other, drawers full of cold cuts and shelves filled with baking staples. Chef Dawn had some mighty good organizational skills.

He grabbed a bottle of water and took his seat at the end of the table. "Water's good for now." He might need something stronger later.

"Enjoy," she said, removing her apron, folding it and putting it away in a drawer. "I hope you like it."

He glanced at the food. "What's not to like? I can already tell I'm going to enjoy it."

"I wish all my other critics were that easy."

"I guess they wouldn't be called critics, then."

She chuckled, and the bright sound filled the kitchen. "No, I guess not." She gestured toward the back rooms. "I'll, uh, just be in my room. If you want anything else, please let me know."

"What? You're not eating with me?" he asked, as if that was incomprehensible.

"No, I, uh…no." She bit her lower lip, and Cade's gaze automatically ventured there. She had a pretty mouth, sort of heart-shaped, and right now she was nibbling on her lower lip as if it were made of chocolate candy. He had to admit she was a looker, with a pretty face and those deep ocean-blue eyes. "I usually don't eat with my…client."

He was her *client*? He guessed that was one way of putting it. "You have things to do?"

"When I'm not cooking, I'm contemplating cooking," she said. "Working on my recipes or doing research."

"Ah, got it. But just so you know, I don't mind if we share our meals. You're welcome to join me anytime." There—he didn't think he was being overbearing, but in this day and age, one had to be extra careful.

"Thank you. I'll remember that."

She walked out of the room, leaving him alone in the kitchen. He took a bite of her food. The chicken was really delicious, with a depth of flavor he'd never tasted before. Actually, he couldn't remember ever having a better-tasting chicken dish. He had to hand it to her, she was talented. And for what it was worth, this time his mother's meddling had done some good. She'd hired a great chef.

He nibbled on the food. It was delicious, but he didn't have much of an appetite lately. He'd lost some weight in the past eighteen months. Sometimes he could hardly believe it'd been that long. His life had been all planned out. He had direction and drive and was looking forward to marriage and having a family. But fate had interfered, destroying his dream.

He rose from the table and rinsed off the dishes, putting them into the dishwasher. He wasn't going to turn Chef Dawn into a housekeeper. He could lend a hand at the cabin. Besides, what else did he have to do for the rest of the day, chop wood?

He laughed at the notion, then walked into the massive living room and took note that the woodpile on the hearth was almost depleted. Damn, now that he thought about it, what better way to kill off the restlessness that crept up inside him whenever he was alone than to do hard physical labor? Yeah, he liked the idea.

Cade changed into his hiking boots and went outside, marching around to the back of the cabin, where he found an ax, protective eyewear and a hard hat in the shed. The old chopping block was right where it had always been. "See if I remember how to do this," he muttered, placing a thick log on the block and lifting the ax. One swing later, he was grinning. He loved the strain in his arms, the pull of his muscles as he landed the second blow and split the log. He hadn't lost his touch. Five logs later, with the sun beating down on him, he removed his black T-shirt and sopped up a layer of sweat from his brow. The sun felt good on his shoulders and back, and as he lifted the ax once again, he heard a female voice.

"Oh."

He swiveled around, ax in hand, and faced Dawn. She was wearing a pair of cutoff jean shorts, a blue-plaid shirt and a pair of tan hiking boots. She looked like a modern-day version of Daisy Duke. As a teen, he'd watch reruns of *The Dukes of Hazzard*, just to catch a glimpse of Daisy in her cutoffs.

"Sorry." She gulped and stared at his bare chest.

She was a good six feet away, but he felt the intimacy of the moment down to his toes. The appreciation shining in her eyes wasn't lost on him. He was grieving, but he wasn't totally dead inside. And just for an instant, a spark passed between them. Something unnamed. Something he was better off not defining. Yet it was there, and maybe it was simply a boost to his ego, having a woman gawk at him that way.

Though she probably had no clue what her eyes were revealing.

"Going somewhere?" he asked.

She cleared her throat. "I'm going for a little hike." It sounded like fun.

"I didn't know you were back here," she continued.

"Yeah, I'm just chopping wood. Need to do something with my time."

"I could find something for you to do," she offered softly.

His brows rose. Surely she didn't mean to sound suggestive, but it had come out that way, and all of a sudden, he was imagining all sorts of things they could do with their time together. He hadn't been with a woman since Bree, eighteen long months ago. He hadn't wanted to go there, but he was here now, and for the first time, he was thinking about sex. With a Daisy Duke lookalike. He put his head down so she couldn't read his thoughts.

"I didn't mean…it's just that there's a lot to do if you like the outdoors."

It was a nice save, and he glanced at her again. "Like taking a hike?"

"Yep, there's some interesting vegetation up there that I'd like to check out. Just wanted to let you know I'll be gone for an hour. So how about dinner at seven tonight?"

"Aren't there leftovers from lunch?"

"There are. Want to have them tomorrow?"

"Sure. It was really good."

"Thank you. I'm trying out a new recipe for tonight. How do you feel about pasta?"

"Who doesn't love pasta?"

She smiled sweetly, glanced at his chest one more time and then turned away, giving him a beautiful view of her long tan legs and perfect behind as she wandered off.

It was something he shouldn't be noticing. But man, he wouldn't be male if he didn't.

Two

Harper had been taking the same hike every day since she'd arrived, because the paths were relatively remote and she didn't run into a lot of people. It was a perfect way to clear her mind without worry of being spotted. Her disguise seemed to be working.

Cade didn't bat an eye in recognition when they'd first met, thank goodness. Lucky for her, he didn't watch much television.

Seeing him just minutes ago chopping wood bare-chested brought thoughts of a rugged lumberjack to mind rather than a big business tycoon. The sight of him holding that ax with his muscles bunching, his dark, straight hair falling onto his forehead, the stubble on his jaw, put her female instincts on high alert. Which, under her dire circumstances, jarred her. She wasn't supposed to be thinking about physical attraction or the way her tummy tightened when Cade wielded that ax. No, she was supposed to be recovering from a scandal that had rattled her entire world, not ogling Lily's sexy-as-sin brother.

The May sun beat down, warming her limbs. As she climbed a rise, she spotted a blanket of wildflowers, their colors waving in the breeze. It was like a pastel patch of heaven. She stooped down and picked the prettiest of them, making another lovely bouquet.

On her way back, as she walked through a cooler area shaded by Texas live oak trees, she found a crop of wild onions along the side of the path. Their pungent scent tickled her nostrils, and she stopped to pick several of them to use in her meal tonight.

When she was done, she gathered up the onions and the wildflowers and resumed her walk, only stopping when she reached a road crossing. It was single-lane traffic on both sides. She waited as one car after another drove by, keeping her head down. For a few minutes there, she'd almost forgotten her predicament. She'd gotten lost in her thoughts, planning her next meal for Cade, but the fear of being discovered reared its ugly head again. Once the cars passed and they were out of sight, she ran across the road quickly then resumed her walk back.

When she returned, Cade was sitting on the porch, wearing a T-shirt—thank goodness—with a book that he didn't seem to be reading in his hand. Oh well, it was a nice afternoon to just be. She would love to join him in that if things were different.

He looked her way as she climbed the steps and rose from his seat. "Hi. What've you got there?"

She stopped long enough to show him. The flowers were self-explanatory. "I found some wild onions. I'll be cooking them up tonight."

"Sounds good. How was your hike?"

"Pretty good. It's an easy path, if you'd like to try it sometime."

"Maybe I will."

"How did the log splitting go?"

"Filled up the woodpile for now."

"I'd like to try it sometime."

"What?" He seemed baffled at her request. "You mean, *chopping wood*?"

"Sure, why not? Doesn't look that hard."

He grinned. "Was that a put-down?"

"Are you being a chauvinist?"

"Are you one of those women that gets offended easily? If you are, I'm going to have to zip my darn lips a lot around you." There was a teasing gleam in his eyes.

"No, I'm not, but I like being outdoors. I like nature and doing things to challenge myself."

He nodded. "Fair enough."

"I don't expect you to stand up every time I enter the room, either," she said. "But don't get me wrong, it's a nice gesture."

"Southern manners, Dawn. That's all. I've been doing it since I was a boy."

"Okay, as long as you don't—"

But it was too late—he'd already reached the door and pulled it open.

"Uh, open the door for me."

"Sorry," he said. "Old habits and all."

She laughed. She had a feeling this was one battle she was going to lose.

"What's funny?"

"Nothing, really. It's just that the last guy I was with wouldn't know a Southern manner if it hit him upside the head." Unless the cameras were on.

"Well, then. I take it he wasn't a Texan."

"No, he was from back East, and he's history now."

Why she found the need to make that point, she wasn't entirely sure. Maybe it had something to do with the way Cade jangled her nerves whenever he was near.

"Can't say as I blame you."

"You'd be the only one who wouldn't," she muttered.

"What'd you say?" he asked.

"Oh, nothing. Nothing at all."

She didn't want to ruin the day by thinking of Dale. He *was* history. If she'd made one right move lately, it was to refuse his marriage proposal. She had no second thoughts on that one. At least she could feel good about not caving in to the pressure. She'd listened to her heart and her brain. Both told her he was a no-go.

In the kitchen, she took a good long minute to wash her hands. Cade followed her in holding a bottle of red wine. The Tremaines had an extensive wine closet just off the kitchen.

"Thought wine would be good with pasta," Case said, grabbing two wineglasses from an overhead cabinet and opening the bottle. "Would you like to join me?"

She was not a big drinker, but a little wine with her meal sounded good. "I'd love to, later with the meal."

"Mind if I do?"

Heavens, it was his cabin, his wine and his family's generosity in letting her stay here. "Go right ahead."

While he poured himself a glass, she moved around the kitchen, gathering up the ingredients she needed for her dish. "Do you like mushrooms?"

"I do. Are they wild, too?"

"I haven't found any in my hikes, so I'm not sure they grow up here."

"What are you making?"

"It's something a bit different—crunchy pasta with a mushroom and herb sauce. Topped with cheese. I've been working on the recipe, and I'm hoping it's refined enough for my cookbook."

Cade sipped wine and took a seat facing her. "Do you have a publisher for your cookbook yet?"

"Not yet, no." She shrugged. "These days if you're not renowned in the business, you have to have a theme, or gimmick, if you want to call it that, to get any feedback at all. Half of my recipes are a little bit outside the mainstream, like crunchy pasta, for instance, so I have that going for me. And I try to keep them as healthy as possible. I haven't come up with a title yet, but it has to hit the mark exactly."

Cade lifted his glass, contemplating. "How about *Daring, Dining and Dawn*?"

"That's pretty good just off the top of your head." Only her first name wasn't Dawn, and he'd just reminded her that she was deliberately deceiving him.

Her only justification was that she was doing this for his sake. According to his sister, he needed this time to relax and be calm. And right now he'd planted himself at the kitchen table, sipping wine, keeping his eyes trained on her.

It made her jittery.

Because she had this undefined attraction to him. And as much as she tried to talk herself out of it— because it was the last thing she needed—she had no real control of those sparks shooting off inside her.

"Mind if I watch?" he asked.

Yes. She minded. She had to keep focused on her dish and jot down notes for her cookbook, not have Cade Tremaine sitting so close, reminding her how he looked stripped down to his jeans. He was Lily's brother, for heaven's sake, and a guy in need of some peace. And from what she gathered, he was still grieving his fiancée's death.

"No, I don't mind at all." She swallowed, hating that the lie flowed so easily from her lips.

"Thanks."

But she didn't dwell on it; she went right into boiling water for the pasta in a big pot. Next, she turned her attention to the mushrooms, using both portobello and shiitake. She cut them into small, even pieces, getting them ready for the sauce. Once the water boiled, she added spaghetti to the pot. She had the computer set up on the kitchen table, and she logged on, making her notes. She dared a glance at Cade, who sat quietly, sipping cabernet, his eyes trained on her.

Her nerves a bit rattled, she finished her notes and closed down the computer. "What book are you reading?" she asked to break the silence.

"The latest thriller. I'm not an avid reader, but it was on the bestseller list, so I figured it might be good. It's called *Wall of Darkness*. Heard of it?"

"No, I'm not a thriller reader. So, you don't read much?"

"No, usually can't find the time. I'm trying to focus on relaxing, and people say reading is a good way to escape. Unfortunately, relaxing doesn't come easy to me. And I can't seem to get into this book."

"Thus, the wood chopping?"

He smiled. "I'll be building a fire tonight."

"Really? It isn't that cold out, but it is peaceful to watch the flames."

"I remember as a kid, coming here in the dead of winter and sitting by the fire, drinking hot cocoa and playing games with my family. My dad was alive then."

"Was he a gamer?"

"He was. My father loved competition, and he loved to win."

"Most people do. Love to win, that is."

"Do you?"

"Of course. I'm pretty good at cards. Poker, gin rummy, Uno, Go Fish. You name it and I play it."

"Go Fish?"

"I'm a child at heart."

He chuckled and sipped his wine again.

She turned away to stir the spaghetti, and when it was done, she lifted the colander, draining the liquid and then dumping the contents onto a round platter. "There, that just has to cool a bit."

She got out a cast-iron skillet next and put in a few teaspoons of olive oil, setting the burner on low heat.

Cade was quiet. He wasn't much for small talk, and she felt the need to carry on a conversation to keep the awkwardness at bay. "I hope you don't mind me trying out this recipe on you. It's probably like nothing you've ever had before."

He took a second to answer, his expression thoughtful. "If my mother hired you, you must be very good at what you do. So, don't worry about experimenting with me. I'm sort of your captive audience."

She turned to him. "But still, if you have favorites or any kind of cravings…"

Something flashed in Cade's eyes for a split second. "I'll be sure to let you know if I have any cravings," he said, expressionless but for the tiniest crook of his lips. Or was she imagining it?

"Well, thank you. I'm open to suggestions. *Food* suggestions," she clarified.

"Ah, got it," he said casually, as if he was teasing

her. But that couldn't be. From what Lily had told her in the past, Cade had been devastated when his fiancée passed and had withdrawn within himself. He held everything inside until he'd nearly made himself sick. So any notion that he was flirting wasn't really plausible.

Which was a darn good thing.

She finished the dish by sliding the cooled pasta into the skillet and cooking it through until the entire batch was browned lightly on both sides, making it crispy. Then she added the tomato sauce, onions and mushrooms, topping it off with fresh basil and dabs of ricotta cheese. "Are you ready?" she asked Cade as she lifted the skillet from the stove.

"Looks delicious," he said. "You are joining me for this, right?"

"Only if I'm not intruding."

"Food tastes better when shared," he said, his brows gathering. "I read that somewhere."

A little laugh escaped her. "I think that's my line, Cade."

She set the steaming skillet down on the table and then brought over two plates and utensils, quickly setting the table. "Oh, I almost forgot." She grabbed a vase filled with the new batch of wildflowers she'd picked today and positioned it in the center. After a quick assessment of the table setting, she sat down.

The May sun lowered on the horizon, casting a pretty golden glow in the room. It was soothing, and she always loved this time of day.

"My stomach's grumbling," Cade said. "Either I'm real hungry or your food is appetizing as hell."

"Or both. Can I serve you up a portion?" She put out her hand for his plate.

"Sure," he said, setting it in her hand.

She gave him a very generous helping. "I'm not sure if I'm that hungry," he said.

"I have faith in you."

"Do you now?"

"Yes, you look like a man who can really pack it in." She smiled and took her seat, placing a napkin on her lap. She forked into the dish and took a bite, then immediately critiqued her work. "It could use more seasoning," she said. "I'll have to add that to my notes."

Cade had a mouthful of food, and after he finished chewing, he said, "Tastes fine to me."

"It's passable, but not perfect."

"Are you a perfectionist?" he asked.

"When it comes to meal preparation, I am."

"So, you're like an artist. You are your own harshest critic."

"I suppose. I never thought of it that way. I think everyone is a perfectionist about something, don't you? I mean, if you're into fashion, you're probably not satisfied until your outfit totally rocks. If you're a golfer, you aim for that hole in one. So, what is it that you want perfection in, Cade? Your business?"

"Hardly. My business is about the bottom line, but I don't need perfection in that. Only good stats while delivering good product. There are hits and misses in ranching and oil but as long as the Tremaine name stands for honesty and integrity, I'm happy." He lingered on the question a minute. "I guess I found perfection in my fiancée. Yeah," he said, nodding his head. "Bree was perfect, and I think that's all I needed. And wanted."

"I'm sorry you lost her."

He snapped his eyes to hers. "How did you know?"

Oh no. She'd been caught. She'd let her guard down, and now she had to think fast. "Oh, uh…your mother mentioned it. It was part of the interview. She told me you weren't eating well and that I should remedy that. I asked her why and she told me."

Oh boy, what a whopper of a lie. But she'd let it slip and now she had to pay the price. She hoped Rose Tremaine would forgive her, because Harper really wasn't trying to sabotage her relationship with her son.

"My mother told you I wasn't eating well because of Bree? What else did she tell you?"

"Only that. Well, she did mention something about your…your—" She briefly squeezed her eyes shut. Why on earth did she keep on talking?

"My what?"

His gaze swooped down on her like a predator's. She felt trapped and had to answer now. "Your blood pressure," she squeaked.

A tic worked in his jaw, and he gave his head a shake. "That's unbelievable. I'm thirty-three years old and my mother still thinks I'm a kid. The only reason I came up to the cabin was to get her off my back. If I stayed home, she would've been hovering like a damn helicopter."

She shrugged. "That's what mothers do, I guess. Out of love."

"Yeah, I know." He gave her a look, his dark eyes assessing her, as if sizing her up. It was reminiscent of her latest reality show fiasco, being judged unfairly by Team Dale, his loyal fans.

"I'm really sorry," she said, meaning it from the bottom of her heart. Cade had been robbed of the kind of love she'd been looking for. The kind her mom and dad had. The kind that makes you do stupid things, makes you smile all day long, makes your heart sing, because you have a secret nobody else has.

Cade's eyes softened. "You know what? You're innocent in all this," he said. "I shouldn't take it out on you because things didn't work out for me the way they should have."

Oh man. She was so not innocent. She'd told him lie after lie, and it wasn't like her. She hated this game she was playing, but it was too late to back out now.

"Don't worry about it. So, about that wood you chopped today. Still planning on having a fire tonight?"

"I…uh, yeah. I'll build a fire."

He seemed a little baffled by her change of subject.

"While you do that, I'll just clean up in here. Are you finished? Want some more?"

"It was great, but no, thanks. I'm full."

"Too full for a cup of coffee?"

"Actually, that sounds good."

"Okay, well, you go build the fire. Coffee should be ready in a few minutes."

He looked around the kitchen. "Need some help in here first?"

"Nope, I've got this."

"Okay, thanks."

He walked out of the room, and Harper hugged herself around the middle as she shivered. The air was growing colder outside, but that wasn't it. She'd just dodged a bullet, lying through her teeth to Cade. "You have to be more careful, Harper," she muttered. "Or you're gonna blow it for him." The best thing she could do was to get out of Cade's way and let him deal with his issues himself.

The living room felt more like a rustic cabin than any other place in this house. It was a large area, with polished wood flooring and a smooth stone fireplace that reached a steep ceiling. Wood beams crisscrossed overhead, and three good-size sofas formed a horseshoe facing the fireplace. Cade was just finishing up at the hearth, and she watched from behind as he started the fire. "You're good at that."

"I was a Boy Scout," he said, using a poker to arrange the wood as a slow flame began to burn.

"And I was a Girl Scout back in the day, which means I know how to make s'mores."

"Oh yeah? Do you use fancy ingredients to step it up?"

"There's no improving on s'mores. They're just right the way they are."

He rose, dusting off his jeans, and faced her. "I agree."

"Here's your coffee," she said, handing him a mug. "Do you take cream or sugar?"

"Just black is fine. Have a seat," he said, waiting like a gentleman for her to sit down.

"Oh, um. I wasn't going to impose. I have work to do. I should probably get to it."

"You're not imposing. Have a seat and enjoy the fire, won't you? At least while you're drinking your coffee." He pointed to the hearth. "It's gonna be a beauty."

She got the feeling Cade didn't like being alone. Either that or he was just being polite. But her instincts told her he was lonely. Which pretty much sealed the deal, because he looked like he really wanted the company.

"Okay, sure. Thanks."

She took a seat facing the fireplace, and he sat down adjacent to her on another sofa. "This is a nice room. It's big, but it's sorta cozy, too."

He sipped his coffee and faced the fire. "We had some good times in this room."

"That's great. Big families are nice. I'm an only child."

"Oh yeah? Where are you from?"

"My folks are Floridians. I grew up in Clearwater."

The sun had set now, and firelight illuminated the room. The fire crackled and sparked. It was peaceful, sitting here, watching the flames begin to bounce, sipping coffee. Talking to Cade.

"My baby sis, Lily, used to sit on the hearth, fascinated by the fire. We were always telling her to back up a bit, she was too close. Until one day, a spark flew onto her sweater and singed it pretty dang bad. She cried her little eyes out."

"Oh my gosh, that's awful."

"It was scary. But Lily always did have an adventurous spirit."

She couldn't sit here and pretend not to know Lily. She wasn't that good of a liar. And she felt guilty deceiving Cade. She guzzled her coffee down in three big gulps and rose from the sofa. "Looks like I'm finished."

He stood up, too. "Already?" Cade gazed into his nearly full coffee cup. "I'm just getting started."

"I really should get to my work. There's more coffee in the kitchen, if you'd like."

"I'm fine."

"Okay, then I'll shut the coffee maker off. Good night, Cade."

"Night," he said, eyeing her with that dark, sexy gaze. "Sleep well."

"Uh-huh." She scampered out of the room, trying not to raise Cade's suspicions.

Lily had made it sound so simple, but being Cade Tremaine's personal chef was harder than she thought it would be.

And that was no lie.

It was almost nine when Harper's phone rang. She'd gotten into her pajamas and was on the bed with her laptop, inputting notes. She looked at the screen, and seeing Lily's image pop up, answered quickly. "Hello," she whispered.

"Hi. Why are you whispering? Are you with Cade?" she whispered back.

"I'm in my room, and he's in the living room, as far as I know. He's got a fire going in the fireplace."

"Okay," she said in her normal voice. "He shouldn't be able to hear you."

"I know that, but just in case. I'm a little spooked by all of this, Lil. I mean I've told more lies in one day than I've ever told in my entire life."

"Like what?"

"Like what? You have to ask? I'm pretending I don't know you. And that's hard, because he's been talking about you. How you'd all come up to the cabin and play games. He even told me about you singeing your sweater by the fire when you were a kid and how you cried your eyes out."

"He told you that? I'll never forget it. I was scared to go anywhere near that fireplace after that."

"My point is, I made up a lie about your mother hiring me, and it's just gotten worse from there. I hate myself for lying to him."

"It's for his own good. Does he seem relaxed though? Is he eating better?"

"Yes, he's eating my food. But I'm not so sure he's relaxing. He chopped wood around back today, and by the way, you didn't tell me how—" She bit her tongue. She couldn't confess to Lily that she thought he was sexy, especially bare-chested, swinging the ax, with that thick dark hair falling onto his forehead.

"How what?"

"How, uh, he seems to like having company. Every time I make an excuse to leave the room, he seems disappointed. Like he needs me there as a distraction or something."

"Yeah, I know. I think he's afraid to be alone with his thoughts. That's why he works himself so damn hard. And it's also important that you stay there. For you and for him."

"Why for me? What have you heard?" It'd been almost a week since that fateful episode of *One Last Date* had aired featuring her rejection of Dale.

"Are you sure you want to know?"

No. Yes. She needed to know where she stood in the world. "Lay it on me. I can take it."

"Well, the tabloids are saying you went into hiding, and they're calling on fans to keep an eye out for you. I'm afraid they're calling it 'the Harper Hunt' on social media."

She took a deep breath and sighed. Why couldn't this be over? Didn't people have better things to do with their lives than to go on a manhunt—or rather a womanhunt? "So, they haven't let it go yet."

"No, sorry. But they will in time. I'm sure of it."

"I just want my old life back, Lil. You know?" She heard defeat in her voice.

"Hey, you'll get it back, Harper. I know it's just going to take a bit more time. At least you're at peace at the cabin."

"I don't know about that. I'm lying to your brother, seems like every minute of the day. He took me by surprise this morning, and I blurted out my name was Dawn. I know, I'm a fast thinker, but that's the first thing that came to mind."

"Dawn? Well, at least that wasn't a total lie."

"I thought this would be easier, Lily. Honestly, I hate lying."

"It's for a good cause, and to save your own hide. So think of it as a necessary evil."

"I'll try. By the way, I have something to confess." She paused, nibbling on her lip for a second. "I let it slip that I knew about the death of Cade's fiancée and his blood pressure troubles. Let me just say, Cade's furious with your mother. I had to tell him it came up in my interview with her. You may want to warn her and tell her I'm really sorry."

"Will do. Mom will be fine with it. She appreciates you staying there, cooking for Cade. And don't beat yourself up about it, either. He won't stay mad at her for long."

"I hope not."

"Just do your job and try to stay away from Cade. It shouldn't be that hard. It's a big house. Oh, and *Dawn*…thanks." Lily giggled.

"You brat."

"Good night. Sleep well."

She hung up the phone and went back to work on her computer.

She had developed a new recipe for breakfast she wanted to try out. She didn't even know if Cade was a breakfast eater, or what time he got up in the morning. She would soon find out.

Harper had been sleeping unusually well considering she was in a strange bed in a very strange situation. Hiding out from the world took its toll. Maybe it was mental exhaustion, but for the past three nights, she'd fallen asleep and stayed asleep all night long. Feeling safe. Feeling free.

Now she popped her eyes open and stretched her arms above her head. A long sigh escaped her mouth as she enjoyed the first moments of wakefulness. It always took her a second to find her bearings and remember where she was and why she was here.

She slid a glance at the digital clock on the bedside table. "Oh no." She sat up immediately. Eight o'clock! "Oh no, no, no."

The scent of coffee brewing hit all of her alarms. Cade was up already, apparently making his own coffee.

She ran to the bathroom, scrubbed her face clean, tossed on her bathrobe, then dashed out of the bedroom. "I'm sorry, I'm sorry," she said as she entered the kitchen. "I overslept."

Cade stood by the coffee maker, sipping coffee casually, like he didn't have a care in the world. His facial scruff was darker today, and his hair unkempt, yet no one would call it bedhead. He must've won Best Hair in high school, because even unruly, it looked fashionable…and sexy. Oh boy, she had to stop thinking of her dear friend's brother in those terms. It was a big no-no in the unwritten Book of Best Friends.

"Nothing to be sorry about, Dawn. I like to get up early." He flashed her a good long look that made her stomach ripple. "You didn't have to rush out of bed."

She could feel the heat rising up her throat. She'd forgotten her appearance. While he looked hot in a clean white T-shirt hugging his biceps, she was in a ratty robe and frumpy pajamas she'd purchased in town on her first day here.

"I know I must look a mess. I usually don't oversleep like this. Hang on and I'll fix your breakfast."

"First off, you don't look a mess."

She rolled her eyes dramatically, which put a smile on his face. "Okay, but you're not a hot mess," he amended.

No, he was the hot one. "I see the distinction."

He chuckled. "Actually, I'm not hungry right now. Coffee's fine. Well, at least I tried."

She poured herself a cup and sipped. "Not bad," she said. It really wasn't awful. So, he could make coffee and boil an egg.

He returned her nod, his dark lashes framing his eyes beautifully. "Coming from you, I'll take that as a compliment."

A bit of sunshine poured into the window, warming up the room. "I apologize for oversleeping, I should've asked you yesterday what time you like to eat breakfast." Her personal chef skills were sorely lacking.

"I can eat, or I don't have to eat," he said, taking another sip of coffee.

She warmed her hands around her cup. "If you don't mind waiting, I'll go get dressed and make you something to eat. It's a quick recipe. Shouldn't take too long. Is there anything you don't like?"

He didn't hesitate. "Liver, pig's feet, octopus."

She smiled. "I can assure you breakfast doesn't include any of those things."

"Good to know."

"Enjoy your coffee, Cade. I'll have something edible for you in half an hour."

"Sounds good."

She turned to the oven, adjusting the digital dials. "I'll just preheat the oven and be back in a jiff."

She walked out of the room, feeling like an idiot. She'd never been anyone's personal chef before. After culinary school she'd catered for a time, and then she got the head chef job at Perfect and Pure in Barrel Falls.

Ten minutes later, after she'd showered and dressed, she walked back into the kitchen feeling almost regal in jeans and a cocoa-brown tank top, her hair combed and almost dry.

"That was quick," Cade said, looking up from the kitchen table and giving her a once-over. He'd been reading something on his phone, and the minute she walked in, he shut it down. "You look real nice."

"Thanks."

"What's for breakfast?"

"It's a surprise. A healthy take on a very delicious dish. Are you game?"

"Do I have a choice?"

"Of course you do."

"I'm kidding," he said, though he wasn't smiling. He rarely did.

"This recipe is going into my cookbook. So I want your honest take on it."

"I can do that. Don't let me interrupt what you were doing."

"I won't." Yet he didn't turn his phone back on. Instead, he watched her move around the kitchen, giving her his full attention. She tried not to let it bother her, tried to go about her business.

She sprayed and buttered a casserole dish. Then she measured out bread crumbs and flattened them into the bottom of the dish. She set it in the oven and let that cook while she diced up onions, broccoli and spinach and added in a half cup of bacon pieces. While that was sautéing, she separated two eggs, putting the whites into a bowl. Next, she added two more eggs and beat them until they were blended.

She looked up and met Cade's eyes. They were filled with questions, and she felt like she had to break the silence.

"Do you have any plans today?" she asked as she pulled the casserole dish out of the oven.

"I thought I'd take a hike."

"Good idea. I enjoy hiking. You can get adventurous out there." She dumped the mixture into the casserole dish and then added the eggs and topped it off with cheese. "I'll be taking a hike later this morning, too," she said, putting the casserole back in the oven on high heat. Then she turned and went to get something from the fridge.

"Oh yeah? Want some company?"

Her eyes went wide. It was a good thing her back was to him. She'd just stepped in it. She was supposed to steer clear of him, but she unintentionally sounded like she was hinting that they should go together. "Don't you want to explore alone?"

She saw him shrug out of the corner of her eyes. "Do you?"

He'd tossed it right back into her lap, and she couldn't very well refuse him now. She couldn't use work as an excuse. She'd already admitted she was going on a hike. She reminded herself she was actually here by his family's good graces and it was saving her hide. She'd have to be careful around him and keep her mouth shut. "I suppose we can go together," she said, heading back to the stove.

"I'll try to keep up," he said, his eyes twinkling.

She held back a smile. He was teasing her and she liked it—a very bad sign.

She put the bowls in the sink and began cleaning the kitchen. When the oven timer dinged, she put on her oven mitts and pulled the casserole out.

"Breakfast is ready." She laid the dish on a trivet in the center of the table.

"Wow, that looks impressive," he said. "Is that a quiche?"

"Sort of. It's my interpretation of a healthy quiche,

with lots of veggies. But the key is, the bread-crumb layer at the bottom replaces a ton of carbs we would've had with a butter crust. There's some bacon and low-fat cheese in there, so it's not a total loss."

"Well, it looks amazing."

She cut into the dish, placing a large piece on Cade's plate. "Here you go." She sliced herself a smaller piece and was about to exit the room.

"Where are you going?" Cade asked.

She pointed to the door. "I was just going to, uh—"

"Dawn, sit down. Please. I thought we established that food tastes better when shared."

"I'm working for you, Cade. And, well, I bet you don't share your meals with your housekeeper at the Tremaine house."

"Irene has been making our meals since I was a kid. She practically raised all of us, and she always took a seat at our table. True story."

"Really?"

"She's like part of our family."

"But surely, I'm not—"

"My mother hired you, not me. So technically you don't work for me."

"Oh, is that how it works?" She put her hands on her hips. Cade was trying so darn hard to keep her near. She thought she understood why: he hated to be alone with his grief.

"Yeah, that's how it works. If we're going to be here together, we might as well agree to a casual friendship."

"A casual friendship?"

"Why not?"

Well, he'd stumped her there. "But we don't really know each other very well."

"And we can keep it that way if you want. Lord knows I don't like talking about myself, but I don't want you to feel you have to leave the room every time I enter it."

"I don't do that," she said without much conviction.

"Don't you?"

Her shoulders slumped. "Okay, maybe I do. I just want to give you space." What could she say? She'd never been a personal chef before, and she didn't know the rules. But one thing she did know—she didn't want to blow this.

"How about, if either of us need space, we tell each other."

"I can do that."

"Good, then it's settled," he said.

"Okay, Cade." She sat down at the table with her food. "Let's eat while it's hot. Remember, I want your honest opinion."

"That's all I know how to give."

She knew that about him already. But her? She'd been lying to him pretty much since the moment they met.

Three

"You gave me a ten out of ten, Cade. You didn't have one thing negative to say about the casserole," Harper said as she walked beside him along the path leading away from the cabin.

"I ate two helpings. That should tell you something."

"So, you think it deserves to be in my book?"

"Your unnamed cookbook? Yeah, you should put it in there. What's it called anyway? Quiche Dawn?"

She smiled. "I wouldn't name it after myself. My ego isn't that big, Cade," she said, walking past him to master an incline.

He wasn't far behind. And every so often, when she turned unexpectedly, she'd catch him checking out her legs. He'd avert his gaze immediately, but she knew. Now, *that* was good for her ego, and it proved that maybe he was coming out of his grief a little bit.

When Cade had suggested they have lunch on the hike, she'd loaded his backpack with a few items, and now he looked like a bona fide hiker with the pack on his back. Both wore sunglasses and hats, which served her well, adding to her disguise.

As she reached a plateau at the top of the incline overlooking a field, she waited for Cade. "You have to see this," she said.

Cade was beside her instantly, their shoulders nearly touching as they gazed out upon an array of brilliant pastel wildflowers. It stretched on for acres, it seemed, and it was Harper's favorite part of her hike.

"Isn't it beautiful?" she asked Cade.

"It is. It's called *Manta de Flores Silvestres*, blanket of wildflowers."

She turned to face him. "You know about it?"

He nodded. "I've been here once, a long time ago when I was a boy. I guess I'd forgotten about it. But it's something you don't see every day."

"It's breathtaking. Aside from the bluebonnets, which are in abundance, there's so many other varieties out there. I wish I had my camera. And I keep forgetting my phone."

"Well, hold on. I've got mine." He took his backpack off and grabbed his phone. "Smile."

"Oh no. I don't want to be in the picture. I'll ruin it." She backed up, getting out of camera range quickly, and stumbled on a rock behind her. She lost her footing and began falling backward.

He grabbed her immediately, pulling her up, and the momentum from his strength landed her right smack up against his chest. His arms wrapped around her, securing her body.

"Whoa, there," Cade whispered. "Are you okay?"

His lips brushed her forehead, and her heart raced much faster than when she was falling. He was hard all over, his chest a piece of granite, and being held in his strong arms made her feel amazingly safe. She hadn't felt this safe since, well, before she became a star of *One Last Date*. "I—I think so."

Yet she clung to him, closing her eyes, relishing the security of being in his arms. He held on to her without moving, without trying to back away. They were locked in place and time, and neither of them seemed to want to move.

"Dawn," he whispered, his voice tight.

She was well aware that she was plastered up against his body, chest to chest, hips to hips, thighs to thighs. "Hold me just a little longer, Cade."

He tightened his grip on her, and she relaxed against him. She didn't want to think about the ramifications of this little slipup. She didn't want to have to explain what she was doing. She only wanted to feel sheltered and secure, and Cade was providing that.

It was beautiful up here, the air fresh, the peaceful solitude of the moment calming her. But then, things began to change. She felt the pounding of Cade's heart, the tightening of his body. The calm that she felt disappeared, and suddenly her body reacted in kind, heat swarming her, sensations of desire gripping her. She didn't mean to do this to Cade, to herself, but now that it was happening, she couldn't find the means to stop it.

And so, when Cade put a finger under her chin and she lifted her eyes to his, she found hunger and want reflected back at her. "Cade," she whispered.

"I'm gonna kiss you, Dawn. Fair warning."

And when she didn't protest, didn't back away, he tenderly cupped the sides of her face and brought his mouth down on hers. It was a beautiful, soul-searching kiss, his lips firm yet gentle. A deep moan rose from her throat. Her body tingled, and everything female about her stood at attention. Cade kissed her and kissed her, and in the kiss she felt him casting aside those months of grief and solitude while she was forgetting about her own demons, at least for the moment.

"This is crazy," she said softly between kisses. "We barely know each other."

Cade didn't disagree or try to explain their actions. "I know," he whispered.

And then they heard voices; a group of hikers were coming up the path. Both of them backed off at the same time, and they stared at each other. There was regret in Cade's eyes, in his expression, but silly her, she couldn't figure out if it was because he was sorry the kiss had happened or he was regretting the interruption.

Either way, Harper wouldn't want to change a thing. She'd needed the comfort Cade had given her, and she'd needed his kisses, too.

"Hey, folks," one of the male hikers said, coming up the incline. "Is this the right place? Is this *Manta de Flores Silvestres*?"

"This is the place," Cade answered.

"Thanks," the man said, waving on his group. "It's up here, guys."

Cade picked up his backpack and took Harper's hand. "Let's go."

"Hey, don't let us chase you away," the hiker said.

"It's okay, we're done here," Cade answered.

He led her away from the wildflowers and then stopped when they reached a tall Ashe juniper tree, the thick grass underneath lush and green. "Let's sit."

She didn't argue. She had no idea what was going on in his head.

"Okay."

Both of them sat down on the grass. He removed his backpack and took out a small, thin cloth to serve as a tablecloth. She helped by taking out the sandwiches she'd prepared: turkey and bacon on Italian bread with an aioli dressing, accompanied by homemade potato chips. There was bottled water in the pack, and she handed him one. "Are you hungry?" she asked.

He shook his head and unscrewed the cap, looking away from her. Then he finally asked, "What was that about back there?" Then as if he realized it was a bit presumptive to put all the blame on her, he added, "I didn't see any of that coming, did you?"

"No." Although she was extremely attracted to him. "I didn't see it coming, either. But just know, I've had a rough few months lately. I don't like talking about it, but my last breakup was bad and I was deeply hurt." She shrugged. "I guess I needed some comfort, and having you hold me made me feel safe for the first time in a long time. But I didn't mean to start—"

"You're not to blame, Dawn. I didn't mean to imply that. It just came out of left field. I haven't so much as touched a woman, much less kissed one, since Bree died. I guess I needed the comfort, too."

But there'd been desire, too. She'd felt it. It was hard not to notice his body tightening, hardening, reacting to hers. If those hikers hadn't interrupted, who knew where it might have led. Yet if they both refused to acknowledge it, then maybe they could go on as intended. Pretending that they didn't have a physical attraction to each other.

Only now, Harper knew for certain that Cade wasn't going to be an easy man to ignore. He was terribly appealing and boy, did he know how to kiss.

If a way to a man's heart was through his stomach, then Cade was in trouble, because Dawn's meals were delicious, and his waning appetite was gradually coming back. Maybe his mother had been onto something when she'd hired Dawn to cook for him. But that was all Dawn was to him, his chef. Period.

He finished his sandwich, both of them eating quietly, deep in their own thoughts. It was now weird between them after that prolonged embrace and the kisses that shocked his system and stirred his body. Once he'd started kissing her, he couldn't seem to stop. What had started out as innocent had changed into something more serious, a hunger that he didn't know existed within him. A light had turned on, and as long as he could shut it off, all would work out. But could he do that? Could he forget about the way her body felt pressed to his, the soft, exciting crush of her breasts to his chest, the sweet smell of her hair, the delicious taste of her lips? Those few minutes had been heaven, an awakening that went beyond his Daisy Duke fantasy.

Both of them had been hurt, injured in a way that made them wary and cautious, and it wouldn't be fair of him to pursue her. It wouldn't lead anywhere, and he didn't want to add to her obvious pain. He surely didn't want to add to his.

He balled up the foil his sandwich had been in and looked at Dawn. She had barely touched her sandwich. "Do you want to finish the hike?" he asked. "Or go back?"

Her eyes downcast, she gathered up the remnants of lunch and quietly said, "Whatever you want to do is fine with me."

He held back the urge to sigh at her indifference. "I'm up for finishing our hike. Are you?"

Finally, she looked at him. "Yes, I'd like that."

"Okay, then." He helped her repack his backpack,

and they moved on. But there was no more small talk, no more easy teasing between them. For Cade, it was life as he knew it. He should be glad of it, going back to his sullen ways. Only, he wasn't. For a few minutes back there, he'd felt more alive than he had in eighteen long months.

An hour later, they were back at the cabin. "Thanks, that was a good hike," he told Dawn. "We must've gone at least four miles."

"Yeah, it really was," she said as he opened the door for her. This time she didn't berate him or give him an eye roll. No, she simply walked through the opened door and headed for her room.

"Dawn? Are you okay?"

She turned to him. "I'm fine. Just have some work to catch up on."

"All right. I guess I'll see you at dinner later."

"Yes, you will. How do you feel about fish?"

"I love all kinds."

She nodded. "Good to know." She turned and disappeared into her room.

Cade ran a hand down his face. He wasn't looking forward to being alone the rest of the afternoon. What he really wanted was company, preferably Dawn's company. He felt lighter when she was around, less burdened. And he hoped he didn't blow it with her. He'd offered her casual friendship and wondered if they could still attain that.

He climbed the stairs slowly and went into his bedroom. Taking out his cell, he called his mother, but it went straight to voice mail. "Hi, Mom. Just checking in on you. Wondering about the progress of the Able Brothers merger. Call me when you have a minute."

Next, he called his sister, Lily. Funny, but that call also went to voice mail. He left a short message on her phone, too. Gage was impossible to get a hold of, and his best friend, Rory, was out of the country right now.

After showering and getting dressed, he walked over to the window to take in the view, and his eyes drifted downward to the yard below. "Holy crap!"

What was that woman doing? He raced out of his room, taking the stairs quickly, and dashed out the back double doors, reaching Dawn before she took her first swing of the ax. "Hang on a second," he called to her.

The ax firmly in her grip, she lowered her shoulders.

"What are you doing?"

"Isn't it obvious? I'm chopping wood."

"Not like that you're not."

"Why not? Don't you think I can do it?"

"I thought you had work to do."

"I do. I did. I couldn't concentrate."

He cursed under his breath. "It's because of what happened before, between us, right?"

She averted her pretty blue eyes, gazing out on the lake. "I don't know. Maybe."

"Do you want me to apologize?"

"No. That's not necessary." She looked him straight in the eyes. "I'm just as much to blame." Judging from her expression, she really believed that.

"You were antsy so you came out here to chop wood?"

"I wasn't antsy, for heaven's sake."

"Restless? Bothered?"

She did her adorable eye roll, and he tried his hardest to keep a straight face. Otherwise she'd be swinging that ax at him. "Cade, don't you have something to do *inside the house*?"

"I do have something to do, right here. To keep you from injuring yourself."

"I'm perfectly capable of—"

"Dawn, you're not wearing eye protection. That's your first mistake. A splinter can fly up and take your eye out just as easily as I'm standing here."

He walked over to the shed and grabbed a pair of safety glasses. "Here, put these on."

She took them grudgingly. "Okay, I would've remembered that on my own."

"Before or after you took your first swing?"

"Am I getting a lecture?"

"Do you want to keep all your limbs? Because you're standing all wrong. One miss and there goes your leg." He touched his hand to her leg, just above her knee to make his point, but the contact had him momentarily speechless. Soft skin, firm thighs. From that single touch, his body tensed up, and he was reminded of how good her kisses were, how good she'd felt pressed up against him.

He cleared his throat and backed up a step. "Are you sure you want to do this?"

"I am the one holding the ax, remember?"

Cade shook his head. "Okay, fine." He took hold of her shoulders and positioned her, making sure all body parts were out of harm's way when she brought the ax down. "Okay, now, stay focused. Keep your eye on the center of the log—that's where you want to hit. And you have to keep the head of the ax straight to make the cut worthwhile. Ready?"

She nodded. He stood directly behind her, holding the handle along with her. "I'll help you raise it. All you have to do is come down straight."

She nodded. "Okay."

He had one hand on her shoulder, holding her taut, while his other hand helped guide the ax up. "Ready, now."

The ax came down in the center of the wood, only splitting the log partway.

She turned to him, her face inches from his, and their eyes met. He breathed in her scent, something akin to sweet vanilla. He swallowed, feeling the full force of her gaze. "How was that?" she asked. "It didn't go all the way through."

Something bubbled up inside him. Her raw determination mingled with her nearness rattled his nerves. She wasn't a wilting violet, that was for sure. She was a woman who enjoyed the outdoors, someone who liked a good challenge. She was also extremely appealing in this setting. And he was beginning to like her a bit too much. Which wasn't a good thing.

"That was a good try," he told her, helping her yank the ax from the wood. "You needed a little more power to finish the job. Now, just do it again. You don't have far to go and you'll finish the log off."

"By myself?" she asked.

"Unless you want my help?" He pretty much knew the answer to that.

"No, no. I can do this."

This time, Cade stood back and let her take the swing on her own.

She followed all of his earlier suggestions and aced it, the two halves of the log falling to the ground. She turned to him, took off her safety glasses and grinned. "I did it."

Her joy was contagious, and he smiled along with her. "Yes, you did. Though I wouldn't call you a lumberjack just yet."

She didn't take offense; instead her expression softened. "Thanks for your help. I guess I needed the instruction."

He didn't gloat. Well, not outwardly. "Any time, Dawn. Just promise me that you won't come out here to chop wood without telling me."

"You don't trust me?"

"It's for my sanity, okay?" He realized he was beginning to care about her, more than he'd cared for a woman since Bree. "You're still a novice."

"All right. But since you're out here now, how about I do another?"

"Another?" He rubbed his chin, feeling the rough stubble there. "I thought we'd go in and have dinner. I'm getting hungry." It was a ruthless lie, but one he knew would work. If Dawn was anything, she was dedicated to her profession.

"Oh, right. Sure." She put the ax down. "I'll get right on it."

"You go on in, and I'll clean up here."

"You sure?" she asked.

He patted his stomach. "I'm absolutely sure."

Dawn was happy with the way her whitefish tacos turned out. She'd used cod, eight cloves of garlic and half a dozen herbs to give the fish added flavor. She'd shredded cabbage and made a light salsa for the dish. Rice pilaf and fresh cherry tomatoes complemented the dish. Cade had eaten three tacos, raving about the meal, and when they were through eating, he'd lent a hand in the cleanup.

After he left the kitchen, she put on a pot of coffee and waited while it brewed. She'd wanted to bake some sort of dessert, but between the hike, the wood chopping and being totally distracted by Cade and the way he'd kissed her today, she'd run out of time.

So she dug into the pantry, coming up with a box of shortbread cookies. They were perfect to dunk into coffee. She arranged a little tray of them, setting them on the table. Once the coffee was ready, she went in search of Cade. She found him in the main room, sitting on the sofa, a fire blazing in the fireplace. He was shuffling cards and barely noticed her walking in.

The sun was just setting, and there was a briskness in the air. The fire sure looked inviting. "Cade, coffee's ready. Want me to bring it in here?"

He looked up and shook his head. "No, thanks, I'll get it myself."

Stubborn man. He didn't want her to serve him. But it was no trouble. And honestly, doing something for him made her lies to him seem a little more palatable. "Okay."

She turned to walk out of the room, and he followed her into the kitchen. "I found some shortbread cookies and thought they might go well with coffee."

He grabbed one from the dish and tossed it into his mouth. "Good idea," he said, his mouth full.

She chuckled and turned away to grab two mugs from the cabinet. "What are you playing out there?"

He came to stand beside her. "Solitaire. It's no fun, though."

She gave him a look. "Why not?"

"There's no one to play against."

She gave her head a tilt. "Is that a hint?"

"You play cards, don't you?"

"I do."

"It's real nice by the fire. We could play while we drink coffee."

"And dunk cookies?"

"Yep, that, too."

It did sound like fun, and as long as they were pretending nothing happened between them today, it could work. "Sure, maybe for a little while."

Cade picked up the dish of cookies and his coffee and walked to the sofa. She followed him, sitting on the opposite sofa, a clear glass coffee table separating them. She was wearing shorts and a short-sleeved blouse, so right about now, the heat drifting up from the crackling fire warmed her bones.

"What do you want to play?" he asked, grabbing the deck of cards. He was a master shuffler. He had these long fingers that seemed to easily control the deck.

"Rummy."

"Sounds good to me."

He dealt the cards, and as she picked up hers, she groaned.

He glanced at her. "That's not a good poker face."

"Good thing we're not playing poker."

"Remind me to play poker with you sometime."

"I can bluff with the best of them, Cade. Don't you worry."

She sipped coffee and dipped a couple of cookies as they played. Both had a second cup, and before she knew it, Cade was ramping up the fire again. He was a fierce competitor, and she didn't like to back down, either.

Cade dropped a seven on the stack, the exact card she needed. She grabbed it and then laid down her hand. "Read 'em and weep," she said. "What is it, ten games to nine now? Guess I just broke the tie."

"I'll get you next round." He pushed the cards her way. "Your deal."

He got up and went to the bar just off the dining room, coming back with a bottle of merlot and two wineglasses. As she shuffled, he poured the wine. "Fortification."

She had to agree, the wine did look tempting. "You need all the help you can get to beat me."

"Don't get cocky. You're only up by one game." He handed her the glass.

"You wanna bet?"

"Sure, why don't we make this interesting?" he said.

Gosh, she didn't mean it literally. But now that the bug was planted, it sort of hung on. It wasn't a bad idea. "What do you have in mind?"

"Best of twenty-five games."

"To be fair, we should start from scratch."

"No, no." He eyed her over the rim of his wine-glass and then took a sip. "We'll go from here. I have no doubt I can beat you."

"And I'm certain I'll win. To prove it, if I do, you have to make me dinner one night."

He shuddered at the thought. "That's more like losing. You know I can't cook worth a damn."

She smiled as she sipped her wine. "You'd have to learn."

His mouth twisted in a grimace. Clearly he didn't like the idea. "And *when* I win, you have to, to…" He stalled, eyeing her body, giving her a once-over that brought thrilling tingles down to her toes. Whatever Cade had in mind she might just enjoy. She sat up straighter, and his gaze focused on her chest. Little did he know her nipples were standing erect from his scrutiny. That one enticing look from him was enough to suddenly turn her on.

Then he gave his head a hard shake, as if clearing

it out. "If I win," he began quietly, "you have to clean out the fireplace every night."

She chuckled and then downed another mouthful of wine. "Like Cinderella?"

"If the shoe fits," he said, and she giggled at his dumb joke.

"Clever, Cade. *Not*."

Then they both laughed as she dealt the cards. She had no clue what time it was. She was lost in the game, talking trash with a fine competitor and enjoying herself far too much. The fire was cozy and warm, and along with the buzz of the wine, she was in a happy place.

She finished off her wine and poured herself another glass. She took a generous gulp, downing half of what she'd poured. Cade's brow rose as he watched her. It wasn't a big deal. He was already on his second glass. Or was it his third?

"I'm fine, Cade," she told him before he even asked. "I'm a big girl."

"I've noticed," he said, dealing out another hand.

She smiled, stealthily admiring him when he was focused on the cards. He was too good-looking for his own good. And with that beard, those incredible probing eyes, he looked absolutely delicious.

She sat there, staring at her cards, feeling giddy.

"Dawn, are you okay?"

"Who's Dawn?" she whispered, then giggled.

"What'd you say?"

"Nothing." Her eyes bugged out at what she'd just spoken aloud. *Shush.* She had to keep quiet about her secret. She took a deep breath to clear her head, but things remained a little woozy. She downed the rest of her wine and set the glass on the table very, very carefully. "I'm g-getting a little fuzzy, that's all."

"On two glasses of wine?"

"Didn't I tell you, I'm not m-much of a d-drinker."

"I'm beginning to see that," he said.

She had trouble keeping her eyes open. She kept blinking and blinking and then felt the room sway. Cade was sitting lopsided on the sofa opposite her.

"Your turn," he said.

As she glanced at her cards, two of them dropped from her hand. "Whoops." She grabbed for them but came up empty as they fell to the floor.

"Okay, game's over," she heard Cade say.

"No, way. I...h-have to w-win."

He rose from his seat, and the next thing she knew he was in front of her and she was being lifted from the couch. "Can you walk?"

"S-since I was a baby." She giggled and swayed, the room beginning to spin.

She heard Cade sigh. "Just hang on to me." His arms came under her, and she was lifted up and cradled, her body brushing the side of his chest. She hung on to him tight, wrapping her arms around his neck, and caught a whiff of him, the scent of wine and musk and man. As they began to move, she stared at his strong jaw, or tried to, because it was really beautiful. "I like your beard."

"Thank you," he said, not too nicely.

"Where are w-we g-going?"

"To bed."

"Okay," she said. "G-good idea, C-cade."

He gave her a stern look.

He walked into her bedroom, and she was gently lowered onto the bed. The mattress dipped a bit as he came partway down with her, her arms neatly wrapped around his neck still. She gazed into his eyes, seeing the dark rims, but seeing something more. "Cade?"

"Shh," he said.

"Are you m-mad at me?"

"No," he said harshly. Then his voice lowered to a whisper. "I'm not mad at you."

"That's g-good. I'm really s-sleepy."

"I know."

He was close still, because her arms remained tucked around his neck.

"I should go now."

She glanced at his mouth. "Yeah."

"Good night." He bent to place a kiss on her forehead, but a cagey devil inside her curved her hands behind his head and pulled him lower, so their lips brushed. Oh boy, he tasted good, his mouth warm and firm against hers. The kiss was sheer heaven. Not a flimsy little kiss like what Dale used to give her on camera, but a deep-down, curl-your-toes kind of kiss that heightened her senses, sobering her up some.

A tiny moan rose up from her throat. "Cade."

He wove his hands through her hair oh so gently, his eyes never leaving her face. "Shh," he said, as if he was in pain.

Then he lowered down on the bed next to her, brushing his lips to hers again and again. It was delicious, the way his mouth moved over hers, how he coaxed her to part her lips and mate their tongues. Her eyes squeezed shut as she enjoyed every single moment of his masterful kisses, the way he swept through her mouth with such expertise.

From there, the kisses grew more urgent and desire swept through her body. She ached for more of him, to feel his body crushed to hers. He made her want…and she was ready to give in, to give up her doubts, to give him whatever he desired.

Her brain cleared long enough to wonder if it was the alcohol making her lose her inhibitions. Or was it Cade? She'd been attracted to him from the moment they'd bumped into each other at the market. All her thoughts rushed together, confusing her as her body stirred restlessly.

And then suddenly the kissing stopped and she opened her eyes to find Cade looking at her with regret.

"I can't do this," he whispered, an apology in his voice. His forehead touched hers, and he inhaled sharply and then rose from the bed as if he was dragged by some invisible force. Looking down at her, he skimmed his gaze over her body quickly, and gave his head a shake. "Sleep as long as you want, Dawn. You'll need the rest."

He walked out of the room and shut the door.

Harper closed her eyes. Her head spun, and she whispered softly, "My name's not Dawn."

Then she got under the covers and rolled over to fall asleep.

Things had to look better in the morning.

Four

The next day, Cade wrote Dawn a note just in case she woke early and found him gone. But he doubted she'd rise early. They'd gone to bed late, and at best, she'd have a headache this morning that would probably slow her down. He'd never seen a woman get so drunk so fast.

He exited the cabin, closing the door quietly. He'd taken a cold shower last night, and this morning he hoped an early morning jog might be just what he needed to purge thoughts of Dawn. Of her pretty blue eyes, her killer body and the way they'd kissed last night. Like there was no tomorrow, like she'd been just as starved for affection as he was. And he hadn't really understood that until their lips met, until she'd kissed him back with such unbridled passion. But he hadn't wanted to take advantage of her last night.

Not in her giddy, sexy-as-hell, tipsy state. She'd had too much to drink, and he'd done the noble thing. Whatever might happen between them would have to happen when she was stone-cold sober and fully coherent, if it happened at all.

He picked up the pace, jogging a little faster now, trying to come to terms with his reaction to Dawn. She was the first woman he'd kissed and touched since Bree. And through his grief and guilt came the realization that he might just be ready to move on. Physically.

But a mental battle was going on inside his head. Dawn was a Tremaine hire, even if he wasn't really her boss. And she certainly hadn't come here for romance. Hell, no. She'd been in a bad relationship recently, and hooking up with him would probably be the last thing she wanted. He was pretty sure he could keep his distance. But a little bug in his head wondered if that was even plausible. They were together 24/7 at the cabin. And he was, heaven help him, attracted to her.

He jogged past a few cabins and came across some other runners heading his way. "Morning," he said, giving them a nod as they jogged past. He slowed as he approached Bright Market and then stopped at the threshold to wipe his brow. He entered and was greeted by a cashier wearing a bright green apron. "Good morning," she said. "Welcome."

"Morning. Can you tell me where you keep your aspirin and tomato juice?"

"Sounds like someone's in need of quick therapy," the woman said with a little smile.

"Something like that."

"You'll find what you need in aisles seven and ten."

"Thanks."

He found the items easily enough and also picked up some packaged chocolate doughnuts and two boxes of crackers. He got in line behind a young boy buying candy. The kid dumped all of his change onto the counter, counting out quarters, dimes and nickels.

Cade stood patiently waiting; he was in no rush to get back to the cabin. And while he waited, he scanned over the rack filled with tabloids. His famous brother, Gage, sometimes made it into those papers. The sleazy reports were never accurate, and Cade certainly had no use for them. But one headline caught his eye, only because it was about a chef. The headline read, Chef Murphy on the Lookout for His One Last Date. Harper Hunt Is Still On. Whatever that meant. The guy in the photo looked dismayed. Cade couldn't believe people went on a TV show to find love. In, what, ten weeks or something? He wasn't sure because the only TV he watched had to do with sports, period.

The cashier rang up his items and he was off again, sort of dreading facing Dawn this morning. He wondered how much she remembered about last night. And he also wondered if he would ever be able to forget it.

It was quiet in the house when he entered and stood in the foyer to remove his shoes. If Dawn was sleeping, he didn't want to rouse her. He tiptoed into the kitchen and set about making coffee as quietly as possible. Then while it brewed, he walked into the living room and cleaned up the wineglasses and cards that were left on the table. It was a big reminder of how things had gotten out of hand so quickly. Dawn had been fine one minute, but after the second glass, she'd gotten smashed in the blink of an eye. What happened afterward was his fault. He shouldn't have kissed her. It was a dumb move and one he wished he could take back.

He set the glasses and mugs in the dishwasher and then stared out the kitchen window to the rustic landscape, where juniper trees were in abundance and the bright sun reflected on the lake water. He had yet to go down there, to check out the lake.

Once the coffee was finished brewing, he poured a cup and sipped. It was hot and burned his tongue. "Crap." That's when he decided he needed a lift. He dipped into his grocery bag and came up with a chocolate doughnut. He demolished it in three big bites, enjoying every second of it.

It was after ten and Dawn hadn't come out of her bedroom yet. Was she okay? Did he dare peek in on her? He had told her to sleep as long as she needed to, but now he worried that she'd gotten sick. The last thing he wanted to do was go into her bedroom and disturb her sleep and privacy. Instead, he poured more coffee into his cup, put his shoes back on and walked out the door. He'd give her another hour to rest before checking in on her.

The lake was only thirty yards away, so he headed down there and walked out onto a small dock they shared with a few other families. It was a beautiful day for a boat ride. Too bad their boat was in storage several miles from here. Cade sipped his coffee, gazing out, watching the blue jays flit from branch to branch, tree to tree, listening to the leaves rustle as they moved. He found a moment of peace here.

The sound of footsteps on the dock surprised him and he turned to find Dawn just a few feet away, her shoulders slumped, her hair barely combed and those pretty blue eyes downcast. She stopped and met his gaze.

"I'll resign if you think it's best."

Harper didn't mean to sneak up on Cade. She'd deliberately made noise as she walked toward him on the dock. He must've been deep in thought, not to hear her until she got pretty close.

"Dawn, how're you feeling this morning?"

"I'll survive," she said. Though she had a killer headache and her tummy ached. She mustered the courage to look him in the eyes. "I'm sorry about last night. About missing this morning's meal. About everything. I meant what I said," she offered softly, only because it hurt her head too much to speak any louder. "I'll give you my resignation, if that's what you want."

He smiled kindly. "No one is resigning, Dawn. So put that out of your mind."

"I would, but it's pretty crowded in there right now."

He chuckled quietly. "Listen, you didn't do anything wrong, and—"

"I'm so embarrassed, Cade. The wine hit me harder than usual."

"It's okay, we've all been there. I got you some aspirin and some tomato juice. Hopefully that will help."

"What would really help would be if last night never happened."

She braved a look at his mouth, remembering his heated kisses. The way their lips seemed to mesh so perfectly.

"We can do that. We can pretend nothing happened. And just for the record, this isn't all on you. In fact, none of it is. I wasn't drunk. I should've known better."

"You're not over your fiancée, I get that."

He winced at the mention of Bree.

"That's not entirely it. I wouldn't take advantage of you, Dawn. Not ever. You have to know that."

"I do," she said, amazed that they could have such a civil conversation about what had almost happened between them. Last night, she'd known the full pull of his magnetism, and she'd let down her guard. They'd had fun playing cards, teasing and challenging each other, and then somehow, the alcohol had sneaked up on her and she'd let her inhibitions go. Goodness, she didn't recall her exact words, but she remembered the way she felt in his arms, his kisses making her crave his touch, her breasts tingling, everything below her waist heating up. And no, he hadn't taken advantage of the situation. "I guess I should be glad you're an honorable man."

"I'm trying," he said, his face pulling taut, and she appreciated his honesty. "Listen, why don't you stay down here, enjoy the lake and fresh air. I'll get you those aspirins and tomato juice and be back in a few."

"You're not making me a Bloody Mary, are you? 'Cause I don't think I could handle any more alcohol right now."

"Nope, just tomato juice. I promise."

He moved past her and headed toward the house. "Cade," she called to him. He stopped and turned to her. "Thanks," she said, giving him a brief smile.

He nodded, blinking his eyes several times, then took off toward the house.

Well, she'd sure made a mess of things. So much for being a professional personal chef. So much for keeping her distance. From what she could remember, she'd practically jumped his bones last night. What had started out as a make-out session could've easily turned into more if Cade hadn't been the adult in the room.

She stared out at the lake, the water looking like smooth glass. It was peaceful here, and she slipped off her shoes, sat down on the edge of the dock and put her feet into the cool water. Lifting her face to the sun, she closed her eyes. In a sense, both she and Cade were seeking refuge in this place. Both were running from something, and both had their own troubles to purge while they were here.

Cade was back in minutes and immediately handed her the juice along with two aspirins. She took them gratefully and sipped the juice as he rolled up his jeans and sat down beside her. He had a bag in his hand. "What's that?" she asked.

"Lunch." He pulled out a box of crackers and some doughnuts.

"Oh man." She put her head down. "I'm awful at my job."

"Don't worry about it," he said digging into the cracker box. "I love these. And they're good for you, to settle your stomach."

"When did you get this stuff?" she asked, taking a cracker from the box.

"This morning. I went for a jog."

"You got me aspirin and juice and crackers?" She choked up, hardly getting the words out. "That's... thank you."

"Welcome. Hey, I have an idea. Why don't we say this is your day off? I can't expect you to work every single day without a break."

"You're being nice again, but you don't cook and I already feel like I've shirked my duties today."

Cade splashed his feet in the water. "You can take the day to work on your cookbook. Or nap. Or do whatever you want."

All those things sounded good to her, but was he trying to get away from her? Was that what this was all about? "And what about dinner?"

"Corky's Bar and Grill in town is pretty good. We can have dinner out for once."

"We?"

"Yeah, we. We both need to eat."

"Right now, eating anything but crackers sounds awful."

"Trust me, you'll be hungry by tonight. And the worst thing for you to do is skip that meal."

She didn't want to argue with him, but she worried about going out in public. Would her disguise hold up?

"I really don't feel like being out in a crowd. The noise and all. Maybe another time?"

"Corky's shouldn't be busy on a weeknight. And if it gets too much for you, we'll leave."

He was pretty adamant. She couldn't argue further without rousing suspicion. He was giving her the day off. She could use the time for herself, to rest, to regroup. She was still feeling out of sorts, and a nap and some privacy sounded really good. "What time?"

"How about seven?"

She nodded and grabbed another cracker, forcing herself to chew slowly and swallow it down. Cade might be right: the crackers just might ease the pain in her tummy, and the aspirin would help with her headache.

"Seven it is."

He gave her a nod. "It's a…" Then he stopped himself.

"It's a plan," she offered.

"Right, it's a plan."

Because it so wasn't a date.

* * *

Corky's Bar and Grill was crowded, and as Dawn stood at the entrance with Cade, she didn't know if that was a good thing or a bad thing. Here in the smoky honky-tonk, she'd either fade into the crowd or risk someone in the place recognizing her. Either way, Corky's was not what she was expecting. She'd envisioned a small, rustic café with few patrons and menu choices, instead of what seemed to be the hub for Hill Country partygoers.

Tonight was live-band night and luckily all eyes in the place were on the front stage, where a singing duo were belting out a Gage Tremaine song called "Rough Night." They harmonized perfectly, and many of the patrons were on the dance floor rocking out to the music.

"Sorry," Cade whispered. "It's usually not this noisy. Didn't know about the band. How's your head?"

She'd rested today, taken a long nap and done some research for her cookbook. "Actually, my headache is gone, and I'd rather it not come back. Maybe we should go? The music's pretty loud."

And she really wished she'd refused him earlier today. Her best form of disguise, after cutting her hair and dying it dark brown, was not to wear any make-up. When she was on the show, she was made up professionally every day. She hoped it was enough.

"I'll take care of that."

Cade handed the hostess a twenty, whispering something in her ear. She nodded and then led them to a table in the far corner of the room, away from most of the people and away from the loud music. "Is this good, Mr. Tremaine?"

"What do you think?" he asked Harper.

She kept her head down, away from the young girl. "It's great."

Cade nodded at the hostess and smiled. "This is fine, Becky. How're your folks?"

"Still going strong."

"Good to hear. Tell them hello from the family."

"I sure will."

They scooted into their seats, with Harper sitting facing the wall and not the band. She wore a jean jacket over a dark blue sundress with tiny flowers, the only dress Lily had packed for her. She didn't know why she'd bothered to dress up, but after she'd seen Cade dressed in a snap-down black Western shirt and crisp jeans, she was glad she'd made the effort. He looked nice. No, nice wasn't the right word. He looked gorgeous, the stubble on his face groomed, his clothes sharp and his thick hair combed back.

"Here's your menus." Becky handed them out. "Let me know if there's anything I can do for you."

"Will do."

After she walked away, Harper asked, "She knows you?"

"She does. Becky's a local. She's been working here for about ten years or so. Her parents manage the cabin for us. They're the ones who stock the place and fix it up when friends or family use it. Becky is putting herself through online college."

Oh, so that explained the big tip.

She glanced at the menu, using it as a shield to keep her face hidden. She had to admit it was nice being out, listening to music and being served for a change. The menu was ginormous. She couldn't decide if she wanted steak, fish, tacos, pasta or chili. "What's good here?"

Cade put his fingertips on her menu and pulled it down, so he could see her face. "Steak fajitas are my favorite. If they still make them as good as they used to."

"How long has it been since you've been here?"

"Oh man. Let me think…must be at least five years or so. Came up here to celebrate my sister Lily's birthday."

Harper pulled up the menu to cover her face again. "That's nice. You know what, I think I'll have the fajitas, too, only with chicken." She couldn't change the subject fast enough.

"Want a drink?"

She glanced at him over the menu, furrowing her brows.

"A *soft* drink," he said. "I couldn't handle anything more."

She put the menu down. "What does that mean, Cade?"

He glanced at her, his eyes roaming over her face and then shifting to the sundress she wore. "Nothing, forget I said that. But you do look very pretty tonight."

His compliment went straight to her head, and warmth traveled through her body. They were tiptoeing around each other tonight. It was safer that way, but she wasn't immune to the charm he probably didn't realize he had.

"Lemonade sounds good."

"A safe choice."

"Funny."

"You know what I was thinking? We never finished our rummy challenge."

"I suppose you think you were winning?"

"Actually, I think we were all tied up."

"Really? I don't remember."

"Trust me. I do. You trash-talk with the best of them," he said.

"I'm competitive." She frowned, hating that he'd seen her less-than-awesome side. "Sometimes, that's not such a good thing."

"On the contrary, I think it's a great trait for people who want to get ahead in their lives, their careers."

"And you would know this because you're a big business tycoon and being competitive is part of the game."

"I'm just trying to stay one step ahead of the next guy, otherwise the company may not survive."

"That's a little drastic, isn't it?"

"Not when you employ thousands of people throughout the country. It's my obligation to make sure they all have jobs. Don't you want to be one of the best chefs in the country?"

"Yeah, but that's only because…I take pride in my work. I set high standards for myself."

"You also don't give yourself enough credit, Dawn.

You're very good at what you do. You're very passionate about your work."

"So are you, at least from what I can tell."

"Guilty as charged. I had two passions in my life, and now Bree is gone."

Just the way he spoke his late fiancée's name said so much about his great love for her. Harper had the urge to reach out and touch his arm. To comfort him for his loss. One day, she wanted to have that same kind of unconditional love in her life. "I'm sorry about that, Cade."

"I had to compete for her, too, you know. She was dating some guy," he said, "who was all wrong for her, and there was, well, a bit of competition between the two of us. She was worth the effort. There was no way I was giving up. And I finally broke her down and made her see I was the only one for her. We'd been so happy, looking forward to the future, until she got sick."

"It must've been hard for you."

"It's…getting better. I think coming here has helped. I might have to eat crow and thank my mom for pushing me into this."

"Well, if you're glad, then I'm glad."

Cade gave her an honest look, one that seared right through her and made her feel more for him than sexual attraction. He was one of the good guys. "Don't take this the wrong way, but I'm glad you're here. With me. It helps."

She took a deep swallow and nodded, unable to conjure up any words.

The waitress came by, breaking the tension of the moment, and took their orders. Harper was grateful for the intrusion because she'd taken his words to heart and didn't know if she could conceal the growing feelings she was having for him. Concealing her identity was one thing—concealing her heart was quite another.

They made small talk during the meal. It was just as delicious as Cade had mentioned. She was happy to see him gobbling up his food. Maybe he was slowly coming out of his grief.

When they were almost through, the band leader announced this was their last song before they took a break. "And folks, it's come to my attention that we have Gage Tremaine's big brother in the house."

Surprised, Harper swiveled her head slightly and caught the lead singer pointing toward them. She immediately spun back around and froze in place. Heads must be turning their way, dozens of eyeballs trying to get a look at Cade. She heard a small round of applause. Oh man, she didn't expect this. Lucky for her, her back was to them. Cade didn't seem to enjoy the attention, either, unlike his famous brother, who always seemed to eat it up. "Sorry," he mumbled to her. "It happens occasionally."

She nodded.

The lead singer went on. "Mr. Cade Tremaine, why don't you bring your little lady up to the dance floor and join everyone else in one last dance?"

Cade was too much of a gentleman to shoot the man down. "Do you want to dance?" Cade asked her.

She shook her head adamantly. "No."

Cade told the guy no with a shake of his head.

"Aw, c'mon," the guy said good-naturedly. "One turn around the dance floor. We'll sing a real pretty song for all of you."

"I'm afraid if we don't, there'll be more of a fuss," Cade said. Then he rose and put out his hand, giving her no choice. "We'll make an escape as soon as we can," he told her.

She took his hand, keeping her head down, her hair in her face. The band didn't start up until they reached the dance floor. "I'm a terrible dancer," she whispered.

"Then stick close and we'll melt into the crowd."

Which was exactly what she wanted. She couldn't afford to be singled out on the dance floor. There had to be at least two dozen couples dancing, and hopefully, they'd blend in. She walked into Cade's arms, and they began moving to the soulful ballad. She caught a few people watching them, and she immediately put her head on his shoulder to hide her face. Cade tightened his hold on her, keeping her within the circle of his strong arms. She'd lied to him once again. She knew how to dance; she'd taken dance lessons all through her childhood and early teens. Her folks had wanted to expose her to all sorts of things to help her find her real passion.

"You're not bad at this," Cade said, his husky voice vibrating through her body. Her cheek brushed his neck, and his delicious male scent wafted to her nostrils.

"I'm trying," she whispered.

Cade moved his hand up to her lower back and tangled his fingers through her hair. The singer's soulful voice transported her. It was magical, a beautiful moment in time. She swayed when Cade swayed, and they moved as one.

She rode her hands up his chest and around his neck and smiled when he looked down, his dark eyes gleaming and his expression open for a change, showing her a side of him she hadn't seen before. "You're beautiful, Dawn."

She batted her eyelashes, not to be melodramatic but because he'd spoken genuinely and she didn't know what to say to him in return. He was beautiful, too. He was a real gentleman, a man who'd been hurt, scarred probably, and who was just, at least in this moment, opening up a little. Knowing that did things to her she couldn't name, but it was a good feeling.

She hated the lies, the cloud of deception she was under. She hated to do that to Cade. He didn't deserve it. Every time he called her Dawn, she squirmed. Whatever was happening between them—and make no mistake, there was definitely something happening between them now—she remembered the falsity of their relationship. But she'd promised Lily to stay on here and keep her brother from sinking into a deep hole. Now that she'd gotten to know Cade a little bit, she wanted to continue. She wanted to pull him out of his grief and help him recover. Not necessarily because he was Lily's brother, and not because he was deadly handsome, but because she cared about him from the bottom of her heart. Which was crazy. She'd known him less than a week. But then again, she'd gone on a reality show and had been expected to marry a guy after less than ten weeks. So, she supposed on that premise, it wasn't altogether that crazy.

"Cade, I…like you." That was lame. Was she still in grade school? But it was honest, and being honest with him now was just what she needed to do.

He brushed his lips to her hair, just above her ear, in that place that brings tingles. "I like you, too."

He pulled her closer, and she immediately understood just how much he did like her. Heaven help her, she was as turned on as he was. No lie.

"Can we pretend we just met tonight?" he asked.

She whispered in his ear. "And then what?"

"Then, I bring you to the cabin and we…"

"Play cards?"

He blew out a breath, as if in pain. "After, we can play cards, Dawn. Is that what you want?"

She did. She really did. They'd been denying their attraction to each other for days now. She brought her mouth to his and kissed him soundly, so there would be no doubt. He was delicious all over, his mouth just one of the places she wanted to taste. She pulled away to see hunger in his eyes and feel the heat emanating from his chest.

"Let's get out of here," he said, taking her hand and leading her to their table. He dropped a hundred-dollar bill down, picked up her purse and handed it to her, and together they made a quick dash out of the place.

He stopped once they were outside to kiss her again, his mouth devouring hers. She was so swept away that she remained silent in the car on the way home.

In the house, Cade led her up the stairs, her hand clasped in his. She'd only been up here once before, when she'd first gotten here, which seemed like an eon ago now. He stopped at the threshold to his bedroom and took her face lovingly into his hands, searching her eyes for any sign of refusal, before bringing his mouth down on hers again. The kiss was wrought with desire, filled with hunger. She had to steady herself from the impact of his kiss. Thrills ran through her body, her heart fully involved already.

"I…I didn't expect this." He brushed hair away from her face with the tenderest touch.

"I didn't, either, Cade," she whispered.

Her heart pounded like crazy; everything she'd ever wanted in a man was standing right in front of her. It was inconvenient he was Lily's brother, and that Harper had lied to him, but none of that mattered now. From the moment she'd first met him in the market, she'd felt an immediate connection to him. A spark that only continued to burn bright with every minute she spent with him.

"Come with me. I want to show you something." He led her into the bedroom and over to a trio of large windows facing the lake. He stood behind her, his hands on her shoulders. The moon was full tonight, and the lake waters glistened with a fine sheen under the stars.

"It's so peaceful."

He rubbed her arms up and down slowly, his touch a low-burning flame on her skin. Then he moved her hair to one side and nuzzled her neck, kissing her with tiny little nips. Tilting her head, she gave him more access, closing her eyes. "Are you sure, Dawn?"

She turned in his arms and slipped her fingers under the spaghetti straps of her sundress, lowering them one at a time down her arms. Then she slid the dress off her shoulders and past her hips. It draped down to the floor, exposing her nudity but for the bikini undies she wore. She gazed deep into his eyes. "I'm sure. Are you?"

Cade's lips twitched. "Oh yeah."

He pulled her into his arms, crushing her into his chest. The contact was immediate, fiery and wild. He brought his mouth to hers again as he roamed her body with his palms, caressing her shoulders, her back and then lower. He palmed her cheeks through the skimpy material of her undies, applying sweet pressure to pull her tight against him, handling her like something precious, yet something he desperately needed.

In the back of her mind, she hoped this wasn't just about sex. About relieving an itch. From what she gathered, he hadn't been with a woman since his fiancée died. She didn't know that for a fact, but she assumed. And now, here she was, living under his roof, about to make love to him. Was this only because she was convenient?

His next kiss wiped that thought from her mind. Whatever this was, she was all in. She'd never experienced anything like this before, this need, this craving, to be with him. It was almost unexplainable. But for her, it was real.

The snaps of his shirt were easy to pull apart. It came off quickly and then her lips were on his chest, her hands roaming his upper torso, his amazing rock-hard muscles.

He made her breathless. And bold. And she wanted more of him.

"Dawn," he whispered. And she mentally flinched. She didn't want him to call her that. She didn't want the deception to go on, though she knew it had to.

And then his hands were on her breasts, his fingertips teasing, caressing, until all the nerve endings below her waist quivered. And when he was through tormenting her in the best possible way, he took her hand. "Come to bed with me."

He led her to his massive bed and lay down, taking her with him. She ended up atop his body, her breasts pressed to his chest. He sucked air into his lungs. "You have no idea how much…"

She swallowed hard, afraid of what he was going to say.

How much he needed a woman. How much he'd wanted to do this since he laid eyes on her. How much she'd tempted him.

"H-how much what?" she asked quietly.

"How much better I feel when I'm with you."

Oh God. It was the perfect thing to say, and she couldn't deny that she felt the same way about him.

"Really?"

He blew out a big breath. "Yeah, really."

She wanted to cry from the beauty of that statement. Cade was a special man, and she wanted him in a very special way. "Me too."

He kissed her then, and there was more meaning in his kiss this time. It was different and good. Better than good. It was Cade.

They tangled in his sheets for half the night, Cade caressing every part of her body with equal attention. His tongue in her mouth made her crazy, his mouth on her breasts made her wild, but his mouth below her waist made her cry out joyously. And when he was deep, deep inside her, every pleasure she'd ever known was magnified by a thousand. When he was through with her, she was totally complete, totally sated. She could languish in his bed forever and never get up.

But morning came too early, sunshine spilling into the vast bedroom windows. She woke beside Cade, his arm around her shoulder, her head on his chest. She watched him sleep soundly. He was solid as granite, handsome and virile, but he was also a considerate lover, not satisfied until she'd had multiple orgasms. And just maybe she'd worn him out a little bit last night, too. She smiled, remembering how delicious it'd been to make love to him, to generously give to him what he'd given to her.

She carefully kissed his chest, wanting nothing more than to stay with him, but she had work to do, and she wasn't going to shirk her duties again. She tiptoed out of bed and went downstairs to shower and change.

As she moved, her body ached just enough to remind her of the sensual night she'd spent with Cade. She was sore in all the right places. It'd been a long time since she'd been with a man. Before Dale, she'd been in a few relationships that were all wrong for her. But today, after being with Cade, nothing felt more right. She embraced the aches as a badge of honor. She only hoped Cade had no regrets, because she sure as hell didn't.

After showering, she dressed in her usual uniform of jeans and a cold-shoulder top and walked into the kitchen, her domain. She was comfortable in her surroundings now and turned on the radio, keeping the sound low so as to not to wake Cade. She danced around the kitchen, pulling out bowls and pans, setting the coffee to brew, feeling happier than she had in a long time. She refused to let reality intrude, to make her feel guilty about anything.

But deep down she feared Cade would wake up and think this was all a big mistake. Despite the sweet things he'd said to her last night, despite how he'd held her tight in his arms, refusing to let her go back to her own bed.

"You belong here," he'd said, right before he'd drifted off to sleep.

She whipped up eggs in a bowl and added fresh

bacon bits, diced ham, chopped olives, artichokes and onions, and then grated in a cup of Gruyère cheese. She dumped the mixture into a cast-iron skillet, added a few spices and heated it on the stovetop. Then she set about making honey-glazed corn bread from scratch. She took the bowl in her arms, using a spatula to combine all the ingredients as she continued dancing around the kitchen, humming along with the melody pouring out of the radio.

On her third spin around, she stopped up short, coming face-to-face with Cade. He was leaning against the kitchen wall, arms folded, his drowsy eyes on her. She swallowed, her gaze flowing over his bare chest and his jeans sitting low on his hips. His hair was an unruly, thick mop, the locks falling into his eyes, and the scruff along his jawline was one day darker.

"Beautiful," he said, pushing away from the wall and approaching her. He took the bowl from her, setting it on the counter, then laced his right hand with hers and spun her around to the music once, twice, and then pulled her up into his arms on the third spin, his hands locking behind her waist as he kissed her hungrily on the lips. "I missed you when I woke up."

Again, the man knew just the right thing to say. "It was getting late, and I made us a frittata for breakfast." She poured him a cup of coffee. "Here, enjoy."

"I did. Did you?"

"Is there any doubt?" Didn't he know what a fantastic lover he was? "I mean, I usually don't dance around the kitchen when I cook in the morning."

"It's a nice look on you. You should do it more often. I'll be glad to help with that anytime."

She smiled before she sipped her coffee and liked that they weren't getting all serious about what happened last night. Sometimes you could overthink things, and right now, all she wanted was to feel the way she was feeling. "I'll remember that."

She poured the corn bread mixture into a greased pan and set it into the oven.

"Should be done in thirty minutes," she said, mostly to herself.

Then she took a seat adjacent to Cade at the table and both of them gazed out the window. "It's a beautiful day."

"It is," he said. "You, uh, you want to do something today?" He cleared his throat. "Together?"

She wanted nothing more than that. She could take a day off from her recipe research. "What did you have in mind?"

She trusted that he wouldn't say some cliché jerk thing; she already knew Cade wasn't made that way. He wasn't going to assume anything or force the situation, and she was grateful for that. "A ride? There's some really pretty landscapes around here I'd like to show you."

Her smile stretched wide across her face. "I think I'd love that."

He paused with the coffee cup at his mouth, his eyes gleaming. "So would I. It's a date."

Dating Cade? She liked the sound of that, and it no longer seemed like the end of the world that she was extremely attracted to him.

Five

Harper sat on the cushioned white seat of a ten-guest party boat and looked out at the lake. Warm breezes blew by, ruffling her hair as the boat caressed the lake waters. When Cade asked about going for a ride this morning, she'd assumed it was a car ride, but he'd surprised her by taking her to the main dock, where he'd arranged to have the boat ready.

Now, out on the lake, she felt freer than she ever had. She removed her sunglasses and let down her hair—which was already curling at the ends from the boat spray—just letting herself be without fear of anyone recognizing her. It was glorious and liberating. Here, on the lake, with only a few other boats in sight, she wasn't in any danger of being recognized.

"Over there is where my brother and I would anchor and try to fish when we were kids." Cade pointed to an inlet that was lush with trees and undergrowth. "But the only thing we attracted was a parade of baby ducklings led by their mama. Didn't help that Lily would toss them bread crumbs. She was afraid they were starving."

"Sounds like Lily," Harper said, then realized her blunder. Her heart sped up, and she held her breath.

"What'd you say?"

"I mean, sounds like Lily is…good-hearted."

"She is, but sometimes that gets her into trouble."

The only thing Harper thought to do was change the subject. "I would've packed a lunch if I knew we were going out on the water."

"No need. I got it covered."

"You do, do you? Did you actually put together a meal?"

"Hell, no." He laughed. "I wouldn't subject you to that. There's a little restaurant just around the bend. We can have lunch there, or we can get it to go."

"To go," she said immediately.

Cade gave her a glance from behind the steering wheel and nodded. "To go it is. We'll find a good place to anchor and have lunch on the water."

"Thank you, Cade. This is…nice."

"You're nice," he said, giving her a charming smile. He reached for her hand and gave it a little tug. She went willingly and landed on his lap. "You want to captain the boat?" he asked, his mouth just inches from hers. Her bottom was snugly set on his thighs, and her body quickly reacted.

"Maybe I just want the captain," she whispered.

"Dawn," he said almost helplessly. "I've been wanting you all morning."

His lips came down on hers in a crushing, bruising way, and she couldn't hold back the tiny little moans rising up her throat. He kissed her long and hard, his tongue mastering her mouth, his hands mastering her body. They were in the middle of the lake, alone for the most part, but still out in public.

"Do you want to—"

"Yes," she answered.

He groaned and kissed her again, and she was ready for whatever was to come.

He dropped anchor in the remote inlet, then lifted her off his lap and brought her under the shade of the canopy at the front of the boat. There was a long horseshoe-shaped seating area there, for the most part hidden from view. They kissed again, and then both dropped down onto the cushions, relentlessly touching each other through the confines of their clothes. She ached for more, to be one with him.

When he touched her breasts, she lay back and whimpered. "Hold on," he whispered, kissing her again and again. Then he came over her, unzipping her jeans and pulling them partway down. "Let me do this for you," he said.

And then his fingers were on her, stroking her, and every touch, every caress brought her to the brink. She'd never made love almost fully clothed before, but Cade knew what he was doing. Between his kisses and his caresses, it didn't take long for her little moans of ecstasy to grow louder, fiercer. Her hips arched, the muscles in her legs tightened and then…she shattered. Pleasure flitted around her like butterflies, bringing their beauty and grace. She was devastatingly done.

Cade zipped her jeans and brought her into the circle of his arms, his eyes on hers. There was so much spoken in that moment without words. Perhaps for the first time in her life, she was really in tune with a man. With Cade.

"You still want lunch?" he asked.

She shook her head, unable to speak just yet.

"We'll head back home and finish what we started here."

Yes, she wanted that. Very much.

She wanted Cade, and he wanted her.

It was as simple as two plus two.

Cade steered the boat to the slip by the house and locked hands with Dawn helping her onto the dock. He had to touch her, to stay connected with her and keep reminding himself she was real. She was the balm to his darkness, a woman who had captivated him from the very start. She wasn't a one-night stand or a fluke. She wasn't a woman who wanted to sleep with Gage Tremaine's brother. Just remembering how his touch completely made her come undone on the boat had him becoming a greedy soul, wanting more of that, wanting to keep Dawn close.

Hand in hand they strolled to the front door of the house. He stopped at the threshold and kissed her again and again, loving those tiny whimpers rising from her throat. Reluctantly, he broke off the kiss to open the door. Taking her face in his hands, he searched her eyes. "How are you?"

"Good. I'm good," she whispered in a sultry voice.

"Me too. Now that we're home."

She gave him a pretty smile, and he brought her inside the cabin. He wasn't going to ask her again, or make sure this was all right with her. He'd had his answer back there on the boat, and from her urgent kisses. He led her to her bedroom and closed the door. Her room was smaller than his, her bed a queen, but he didn't mind being in close quarters with her. In fact, he couldn't think of anything better.

He brushed his lips over hers, ran his hand through her hair. "Take off your clothes, sweetheart."

"You take off yours," she answered back.

"Planning to." He unbuttoned his shirt, then unfastened his belt and drew it off with one long pull. He kicked off his shoes, all the while keeping his eyes trained on Dawn as she stripped down to her panties.

"All done, slow poke."

He grinned. "You trash-talkin' me, angel?"

"Have to. You're taking your sweet time."

"You'll thank me later for that."

And then they were on each other, lips meshing, bodies colliding. He caressed every single inch of her skin, absorbing her softness, the supple, sweet body that gave to him so generously. His palms grew hot from rubbing her perfect breasts, loving the firm feel of them, the rosy tips that pebbled up and invited him to do more. He brought his mouth down to lavish one pink tip with love and then the other. She squirmed under his grip and he grew even harder. Gently, he moved her to the bed and lowered her down, her head on the pillow, her incredibly long legs lying across the bed, her eyes on him, glistening like the lake waters.

He sheathed himself with protection and moved over her, lowering down into her awaiting arms. She ran her hands through his hair, rumpling it, then caressed his face, kissed his mouth. They just seemed to fit perfectly everywhere, and when kissing wasn't bringing them close enough together, Cade thrust inside her, his hands on the bed giving him momentum to take her fully, to reach as deep inside as he could go.

Her whimpers met with his groans, pleasure and heat and lust all mingled. "Oh, damn, Dawn," he uttered in a plea. Raw sensations whipped through him as he continued to move, to gaze into her passion-filled eyes. Her reaction to him was his biggest turn-on, the way she seemed to enjoy everything he did to her.

She was not just a one-night stand. Definitely not.

She was scary good with him, beautiful under him, drawing every ounce of passion from him, meeting him thrust for thrust.

"Cade," she whispered, reaching up to his neck and pulling him down for a fiery kiss. She destroyed him in the best of ways, taking all of his breath away.

And then her mouth clamped down, her body stiffened, as she pleaded with him not to stop. And he knew the exact moment of her climax, the earth-shattering second of her release.

Man, he was amazed, stricken to the core. And watching her like that fueled his desire.

He moved harder and faster, and then he combusted, his release an earthquake of pleasure and satisfaction. He rolled off her, taking her with him, to hold her tight. To keep her close. "That was the… best," he uttered.

She nodded, and snuggled his chest.

Where had this beautiful woman come from?

She seemed too good to be true.

After their incredible day together—and even more incredible night—Harper found Cade in the kitchen the next morning. The coffee was brewing, and he was over the stove, burning bacon in a cast-iron skillet. She giggled a little, and he turned, obviously surprised to see her there. "Mornin'," he said. He leaned over to kiss her cheek. "Damn, you look good in my shirt."

"Thanks. What on earth are you doing?"

"Well," he said, sighing in defeat. "I was trying to cook you breakfast."

"Really? That's sweet."

"Actually, it was a very bad idea." He set the spatula down to give her his full attention. Putting out his arms, she walked straight into them. It felt safe there, and right, being cocooned by him, feeling his lips on her hair giving her morning kisses. When she woke up a few minutes ago, she feared he'd left her to sleep in his own room, but instead, she found him here, trying his hand at cooking.

"It's never wrong to cook. If you want, I'll show you how."

"You're willing to teach me?"

"Sure. I'd love to."

"You think you could take me being underfoot all day?" He touched his finger to her mouth, outlining the shape of her lips, parting them with his fingertip.

She drew his finger into her mouth and suckled. "I think I can handle it."

Danger flickered in his eyes. "You are something, angel." His voice turned husky and deep, like a growl.

Uh-oh. She backed away from him and the stove, putting a good distance between them. "I can be a devil sometimes. Especially in the…kitchen. So watch out, bud."

He tossed his head back and laughed, a good, hearty sound that made her grin, too.

Then he pulled her into his arms and gave her a good long, punishing kiss that curled her toes and made her beg for breath. When he was through, her heart was pumping hard.

They broke the embrace simultaneously, staring into each other's eyes. Something amazing was happening between them. For her, anyway. And she didn't think she was wrong in assuming for him, too. But no words were spoken between them yet, nothing more than casual conversation and sexy talk.

Harper didn't want to be the first to make a big deal of it. To put words to their actions. It was better to ride out this thing between them and see where it went.

"So, do you want a lesson in the kitchen or not?"

"I can't believe I'm saying this, but yeah. I want a lesson. Are you gonna tease and tempt me all through the day?"

She grinned mischievously. "Probably. But only if provoked."

"I'll remember that."

Harper showed him how to make the perfect omelet, giving him tips all along with way. She taught him how to chop and dice and julienne. And they danced around each other, trying to concentrate, trying not to touch each other, at least until the lesson was through.

They ate his omelet and drank coffee at the kitchen table as Cade shared some more of his life with her, little anecdotes about growing up a Tremaine. But each time he asked about her life, she had to give him a condensed, measured version, so as not to include the part that included Lily. Or her *One Last Date* fiasco. She so wanted to be truthful with him and hated the lies. But now was not the right time to come clean. Not when their involvement was just budding. She couldn't even call it a relationship, it was too soon for that, but her feelings for Cade were growing stronger every day. She couldn't stop it even if she wanted to.

"The kitchen's a mess," she said after her second cup of coffee. "I'll clean it up." She rose to get started, but his arm snaked around her and tugged, and she fell right into his lap. It was like magic how that always seemed to happen.

"I'll help," he said, giving her a dusky, dark-eyed look.

His cell phone rang, and he grabbed it off the table. "It's from my sis," he told her.

She nodded and bounded up from his lap, her stomach clenching. Thankfully, he didn't seem to notice her panic. She made noise while cleaning up the dishes, and he rose and walked into the other room to have a conversation with Lily.

She was so bad with deceit, she didn't want to know what they were talking about. She didn't want to overhear anything that could cause her to slip up with him. She scrubbed and rescrubbed the pans and bowls, taking out her frustration on them. It was almost as good as chopping wood.

"Hey, you trying to rub the paint right off them?" Cade asked good-naturedly as he strode back into the kitchen.

"What? Oh no. I like to make sure everything gets really clean."

He was behind her and she didn't turn around, didn't face him, but continued washing with the same vigor.

He picked up a kitchen towel and began drying the pots and pans. "You don't have to do that," she said, putting on her personal chef hat. "It's my job."

"I made this mess, I'm damn sure gonna help you clean it up."

There was no point arguing. Cade had a stubborn streak, and a keen sense of duty, she was learning.

"Okay."

"That was my sister. She was just checking in. Making sure I'm being a good boy, eating my peas and carrots. I told her you were a fantastic cook, and I've never been more relaxed. I've hardly thought about work lately."

She nodded, keeping her head down. "Is that true?" she asked softly.

Cade wrapped the kitchen towel around her waist and grasped the ends in one hand to bring her to face him. "Yes, it's true. And it's because of you."

"Me?" She started shaking her head. "Because of…"

"That part's great, Dawn. Don't get me wrong. I mean it, I love being with you that way. But it's also because you made me see how empty my life was before. How I let my grief take hold of me."

"I'm no expert, but I think grieving is actually healthy for the soul. But at some point you need to get over it."

He began nodding, looking at her like she'd accomplished some great feat. "Because of you, I've been hiking, foraging, taking the boat out, learning how to cook. It's like I can breathe again."

She didn't want the praise. She didn't want any credit. She didn't deserve it. "You would've done all those things without me."

"No, I wouldn't, *Dawn*. I know I wouldn't." He

spoke her name softly, with reverence, as if she was a good woman instead of a fraud.

She was trapped by the dish towel, searching the depths of his dark, beautiful eyes. Trapped by his charm, his honesty, his strength. And in that moment, she knew. She was in love with him. Deeply, crazily, stupidly in love with him.

He was the perfect guy. And she was a grossly imperfect girl.

But it didn't seem to matter. Because what she was feeling wasn't going away. She loved him. She loved Cade Tremaine. He was her one last date, whether she wanted it that way or not.

"Dawn? Are you okay? You're blinking like crazy. Got something in your eyes?"

He stared at her, concern on his face.

"No, I'm…f-fine."

He was thoughtful for a while. "If it makes you uncomfortable, I won't speak of it again. I don't want to do anything to upset you."

"You couldn't," she said truthfully.

"I like that you have that much faith in me." He pulled on the dish towel and brought her up close, so no space divided them. The feel of his rock-solid chest made her lose her train of thought. Goodness, they'd made love twice last night, and it'd been amazing both times, but this morning, just a touch, a kiss, had her wanting more. She couldn't tell him she loved him, but she could show him.

"In you, yes. But not in your rummy skills."

He laughed. "Is that a challenge?"

FREE BOOKS GIVEAWAY

2 FREE SIZZLING ROMANCE BOOKS!

2 FREE PASSIONATE ROMANCE BOOKS!

GET UP TO FOUR FREE BOOKS & TWO FREE GIFTS WORTH OVER $20!

We pay for everything!

Complete the survey below and return it today to receive up to 4 FREE BOOKS and FREE GIFTS guaranteed!

▼ DETACH AND MAIL CARD TODAY! ▼

FREE BOOKS GIVEAWAY
Reader Survey

1

Do you prefer stories with happy endings?

○ YES   ○ NO

2

Do you share your favorite books with friends?

○ YES   ○ NO

3

Do you often choose to read instead of watching TV?

○ YES   ○ NO

YES! Please send me my Free Rewards, consisting of **2 Free Books from each series I select** and **Free Mystery Gifts**. I understand that I am under no obligation to buy anything, as explained on the back of this card.

❑ **Harlequin Desire®** (225/326 HDL GQZ6)
❑ **Harlequin Presents®** Larger-Print (176/376 HDL GQZ6)
❑ **Try Both** (225/326 & 176/376 HDL GQ2J)

FIRST NAME	LAST NAME

ADDRESS

APT.#	CITY

STATE/PROV.	ZIP/POSTAL CODE

EMAIL ❑ Please check this box if you would like to receive newsletters and promotional emails from Harlequin Enterprises ULC and its affiliates. You can unsubscribe anytime.

"For later maybe," she said.

"Do you have work to do?" He appeared disappointed.

"No, yes. But honestly, Cade." She rose up on tiptoes, licked at his delicious lips, giving him a mind-blowing kiss. Then she whispered, "The only thing I want to do right now is you."

Cade looked shocked for a second, then he grinned. "Aw shucks, angel. I really wanted to play cards." Then he took her hand and led her up the stairs and into his bedroom.

Cade lay on the bed alone, looking out the window at the flourishing spring scenery. He was in a happy place, the happiest he'd been in a long while. And it was strange that when he was with Dawn, he didn't feel guilty—he didn't feel that same powerful grief that ate away at him.

After they'd made love this morning, they'd dozed off in each other's arms, and now it was approaching the afternoon. Whiling away the time had never been his style, but doing nothing with Dawn was better than doing something with anyone else. His work, the office and all the problems he fixed on a daily basis were what had driven him lately and kept him sane. But not here, not with Dawn. He didn't need those things right now.

With his arms behind his head, he sighed, realizing he'd come to a conclusion. All he needed was her.

The door to the shower clicked open, and he imagined his dark-haired beauty stepping inside and soaping up. Immediately, his body reacted, everything going tight and hard below the waist. He couldn't seem to get enough of Dawn, and lucky him, she seemed to feel the same way about him.

He rose from the bed and strode across the room, entering the bathroom. The glass shower door was too fogged up for him to see anything more than her outline, so he opened the door a tad and peeked in.

"Cade," she said. "You scared me."

"Sorry." But he wasn't, not really. She was covered in tiny soap bubbles, her body glistening under the spray. "But I was thinking I need a shower, too. Want some company?"

He'd never tire of seeing her naked. She had two perfectly round butt cheeks, just enough for him to hold in his palms, a waist he could practically wrap both hands around, breasts that were full and just slightly elongated. Perfect.

"What took you so long, sleepyhead? I didn't think you'd ever wake up."

She had a sassy mouth on her, too, that kept him on his toes. "In about a minute, you'll think it was worth the wait."

He pulled open the door and stepped inside. Hot, steaming water rained down on him, and it felt like heaven on earth. He grabbed the soap out of her hands and turned her away from him, making soap bubbles of his own on her shoulders, her back and then lower, to foam up her beautiful rear end, cupping her cheeks and soaping them, making her sigh restlessly. He came up behind her and reached around to cleanse her breasts, his hands lifting those firm globes and washing them with infinite care.

"Cade," she moaned and turned in his arms.

"Under a minute," he whispered.

"I know. You're kinda hard to resist," she said, wrapping her arms around his neck.

He smiled. If she only knew how much he wanted her. How hard she was to resist. In a matter of just a few days, he'd come to think this woman was his angel. His savior.

She took the soap from him and lathered him up, kissing the places she touched. And then she was soaping him below the waist, her hands working magic on him, stroking him until he was about ready to combust. She was relentless in her quest, and when she replaced her hands with her mouth, Cade couldn't hold on any longer. He couldn't deal with the pleasure she was delivering with her mouth, her tongue.

He stopped her just in time and then lifted her up and carried her out of the shower, quickly drying them off and taking her back to bed. There, he sheathed himself with protection and brought her to the brink, again and again, until both were breathless, sated and spent.

Six

Harper spent the next few days teaching Cade to cook, hiking and boating with him. She was in total sync with the universe, enjoying every second with Cade, every minute they spent in bed and out. In their ongoing rummy game, she was up forty games to his thirty-eight, and she loved teasing him about losing to her. He had a competitive nature and it irked him every time she won. And if she got on a winning streak, the devil in him would distract her with his kisses. One time he actually stopped the game entirely to carry her into the bedroom and make love to her, she believed to end her winning streak. But neither of them minded the interruption. They were hungry for each other morning, noon and night. And when they'd pick up the cards again, each one would go right back into killer mode.

Right now, Harper had a winning hand. She laid her cards on the kitchen table. "Read 'em and weep," she said. "I win again."

"Damn." Cade tossed his cards down. "I was so close."

"Sorry," she said, grinning. She could hardly believe she'd been with Cade one full week. The time seemed to slip by so quickly, and she had no idea how long he planned to stay. How long they'd go on like this, in their own private, sheltered world. Technically, she was here to cook for him for as long as he needed. Lily had mentioned ten days to two weeks, but Cade made no mention of when he planned to return to Juliet County. He also made no mention of his feelings for her. Oh, he was full of compliments, and that made her ego soar. He told her she was beautiful, a talented chef and a kick-ass competitor. But he never spoke of the future. He never mentioned them having a real relationship.

She was in limbo. And part of her was wary of where she'd end up. But another part of her was too darn happy to worry about what would happen next. She was enjoying the here and now way too much.

"My deal," she said, scooping up the cards on the table.

"Hey, uh, Dawn?"

"Hmm, what?" She shuffled the deck.

"I think I'm ready."

She stopped shuffling and gazed into his dark eyes. "Ready?"

"To cook for you. I want to make you dinner tonight."

"Really?" She smiled, noting confidence in his expression as he waited for her reaction. "I'd love that."

He touched her face, stroking his thumb along the line of her jaw. "Thanks for not telling me I'm not ready." He leaned over and gave her a kiss. She loved how when he ended a kiss, he gently tugged on her lower lip with his own lips, as if he wanted to taste every last morsel of her.

"This isn't your way of distracting me, is it?"

"No. Maybe. No," he said finally. "I've been thinking about it a lot."

"What, may I ask, are you making for me tonight?"

"Braised short ribs, with riced potatoes and creamed asparagus tips."

"Wow. I'm impressed. You're shooting for the fences, aren't you?"

"Go big or go home," he said, grinning. "How about we end the game for now? I've got some shopping to do. Wanna come?" He rose from the table.

"Shopping for food is my second-favorite thing to do." Then as he loomed above her, she took in his long, sturdy, muscular body, a body she'd become familiar with in the most primal of ways. A body that stole her breath and made her heart race. "Uh, make that my third-favorite thing to do." She lifted off her seat. "Sure, I'll go with you. And don't you dare ask me what those three things are. You already know."

"I wouldn't dream of it," he said, gripping her rear end with both hands and squeezing gently. A reminder of his sexual prowess, she supposed. But it was working. Every time he touched her, it worked. "I would love to know what position I'm in, though, first, second or third?"

She smiled and backed away from him, giving him a look that said, *drop it, bud.* "We have shopping to do. Ready?"

He nodded, getting the hint. "It's a nice day. Wanna walk to the market?"

"I'm always up for a walk."

The weather was warming up lately, getting up in the mideighties. They hadn't had a fire in the fireplace for the past two nights, and as she stepped outside wearing her usual disguise of a ball cap and sunglasses, the sun's warmth cascaded down on her.

Cade took her hand, and they navigated the two-lane road leading to the store. Harper noticed more cars along the road, more people out walking. It was May and, she supposed, vacation time for students who'd already finished their spring semester. Maybe some folks were taking early vacations to beat the summer rush.

They entered a busier-than-usual Bright Market and scanned the shelves, grabbing what Cade needed for dinner. She helped pick out the best cut of meat and suggested some fresh herbs for the dish. As she was rounding an aisle, a girl who was on her cell phone bumped into her, knocking into her shoulders extremely hard. Harper's sunglasses flew off, and she came face-to-face with the girl and her two friends. All three appeared to be college-aged. "Oh my gosh, I'm so sorry," the girl who bumped her said.

"It's okay. Just maybe next time don't look at your phone when you're shopping." It came out harsher than she intended. But one of her good friends in culinary school had lost her mother due to a distracted driver, so it was a sensitive subject.

The girl's mouth twisted. "And next time maybe take your shades off when you're in the store."

The other two girls were staring at her. Rather than make a big deal out of it, she reached down to pick up her glasses and scrambled to put them back on. Which must've looked weird, since she really didn't need them on in the store and the girl had called her out on it. "I've had eye surgery recently," she fibbed. "Can't be exposed to light."

The girl who'd bumped her gave her an odd look and then the three took off, whispering and looking back at her. It was probably nothing, but a queasy feeling gnawed in the pit of her stomach, and she was suddenly chilled to the bone.

"Everything all right?" Cade came over and put a hand on her shoulder.

"Everything's fine. Just some snarky girls. No big deal."

"You sure? You seemed rattled."

"I'm…fine, Cade." She plastered on a smile and gazed down at his shopping cart. "Have everything you need?"

"You tell me," he said, smiling. "Do I? Oh, you were talking about the food."

She chuckled. He was definitely loosening up, and she needed to do the same. "Looks like you do, both ways."

"Okay, then let's get out of here so I can wow you in the kitchen. Among other places," he whispered in her ear. He had turned out to be such a tease. And she loved every second of it.

"Let's try the kitchen first and see how you do."

"You mean if I get an A grade, I get to wow you in the—"

She put two fingers to his mouth. "Shh, Cade." She looked around. Those three girls were in the checkout line now, and one of them was staring again.

"On second thought, I think we need a good bottle of wine for tonight."

"We have wine back at the cabin, quite a bit of it."

"I know, but you need to pick up cabernet sauvignon. It works best with your dish."

"Okay, you're the chef." He spun their cart around and headed to the liquor aisle. Harper gave one discreet look back at the checkout, noting the girls had left the market.

"You know what, I forgot something," she said. "You go get the wine, and I'll meet you at checkout."

"What'd you forget?"

She smiled coyly. "Body lotion."

His brows arched, and he smiled. "See ya."

She left him, grabbed some lavender body lotion down aisle nine, then rushed up to the check stand, scouring over the tabloids. Luckily, there was only a mention of *One Last Date*, but no photos of her. Apparently, she'd been relocated to page four. All good news.

She breathed a sigh of relief.

Now she could look forward to dinner with Cade tonight back in the safety of the cabin.

"The thing is, once I start preparing the meal, you can't come in the kitchen until it's ready," Cade said to her when they finally got back to the cabin.

"Really?"

"I'm doing this all on my own." He began putting the groceries away. "And later you can tell me where I went wrong."

"Okay, but I have faith in you. You're going to do great."

"You do? You have faith in me?" He set his hand-picked potatoes out on the counter.

"Of course I do."

He rubbed his hand over his chest, looking a bit perplexed. "I don't want to let you down."

"You won't." She reached up to kiss his lips. "Just do your best. I'll leave you to it."

"Enjoy your afternoon off. What're going to do?"

"I'll be in my room, doing some research, but if you get in a bi—"

This time, he gave her a quick shut-up kiss. "Go." He pointed to the door. "I'm good."

"I'm going, and yes, *you are good.*"

She went into her bedroom and caught her reflection in the mirror. The expression on her face could only be described as bliss. Pure joy, happiness like no other. What was in her heart was plastered all over her face. She couldn't believe how much she cared for Cade, how happy he made her.

She sat on the bed and picked up her phone. She'd gotten three text messages from Lily asking for a good time to talk. Since she'd been with Cade almost nonstop lately, she hadn't had time to call. She punched in Lily's speed dial, and Lily answered on the first ring.

"Hi, it's me."

"Harper? It's good to hear your voice. It's been a while."

"I know. It's been…well, I've been spending a lot of time with your brother."

There was a pause on the other end of the phone. "Is this something we need to talk about?"

"Maybe, but first tell me what's going on. I feel so isolated here. In a good way, but what can you tell me about my situation?"

"Well, the search for Harper continues. But it's simmering down. I think. I mean, you're still on the news, but not as much as when you first dumped Dale."

She blew out a breath. "Oh, that's positive."

"It's been close to two weeks now. But that's nothing in tabloid land. They can milk a story for months. Especially a high-profile one like yours."

"We went to Bright Market today. I was fully disguised and I didn't see my picture on any of the front pages. I thought that was something."

"We?"

She ignored Lily's question. "How's your mother doing? And the rest of the family?"

"Well, Mom is doing fine. But now she's worried that she isn't hearing enough from Cade. She thought he'd be checking in every day, bugging her about the business. Giving her grief for making him stay away so long. But he hasn't been calling at all. So, what's up with that?"

"Lily, I, uh. I think you should know, Cade and I are getting along really well now."

"You mean he's not busting your chops, not hating your healthy meals?"

"No. He's been…great. We've been spending time together. Hiking, boating, playing cards. Uh, keeping busy."

"Harper, what aren't you telling me?"

Harper squeezed her eyes shut. She scrunched up her face. "Oh, Lily. I want you to know, I came here with all good intentions. I take my profession seriously, and I was trying to do just that. Trying to be Cade's personal chef and no more. But we're pretty much alone here, and I've been isolated, trying to keep out of the public eye. It started out with us taking hikes together. Then, one day he surprised me with a boat ride, and now we go out on the boat a lot. We have this ongoing rummy game, too, and it's been…"

"What are you telling me? That my brother is having fun? That he's not stressed out anymore?"

"He asked me to teach him how to cook."

"Cade is cooking?" Lily's voice rose to a higher pitch.

"Making me dinner as we speak. It's all his doing. He wanted to learn."

"Wow, Cade is cooking. Having a good time. I think I hate you."

"Oh no, Lily. Please—"

"Kidding, Harp. I couldn't hate you. I love you for getting Cade out of his rut. Sounds like he's coming out his grief. And the two of you are…"

"We're close, Lily. I'm falling for him and I think he feels the same way. I didn't mean to take advantage of the situation. You have to know. It's not a fling, Lil. It goes much deeper than that. I'm in love with Cade. I love him very much."

"Oh, Harper," Lily said softly. "Are you sure? I mean, you just came off that roller coaster with Dale."

"I didn't love Dale. Not like the way I love your brother. He's…amazing."

"How does he feel about you?"

"Honestly, I don't know. We don't talk about feelings. At least not now. But he's happy, and I'm happy. And I don't know where this is heading. But I thought you should know."

"Honey, I'm ecstatic for you and Cade. But there are so many variables. Like, you've been lying to him since the day you met him."

"I know," Harper whispered. Saying it aloud made it seem that much worse. "I've been thinking about that a lot. My conscience has been bothering me. I want to tell him the truth so badly, but I don't want to betray your trust and screw things up. You've been such a loyal friend."

"I don't know what to tell you, Harper. Honestly, if Cade is happy now and you two have gotten close, maybe you should tell him the truth. I think he can handle it."

"You do?"

"I mean, I hope so. But it's up to you. Whatever you decide to do is fine with me."

"And your mom?"

"I'll talk to her. Make her understand. Hey, love is messy sometimes. Mom will be glad that someone new is in his life. That he's come out of his grief. That's big."

"This is happening so fast, and it scares me. But I think I have to tell him."

"Whatever you decide, I have your back."

"Thanks." She nibbled on her lips, contemplating the task ahead. "I'll figure out a good time to tell him, Lil. When the time is right."

The table by the fireplace was all set with the best dishes in the cabin. The wineglasses sparkled, and candles flickered from every corner of the room. Cade had laid out pillows to sit on, and a low-simmering fire burned in the fireplace. The meal was ready. So was he. He wanted to please Dawn; it mattered to him that he would. He'd done this for her, to be a part of her world and show her that he cared.

He didn't know when or why it happened, but he was in deep with her. He couldn't imagine being here at the cabin without her. She'd pulled him out of his slumber and made him see light again. She was pretty and funny and sweet. It'd been his lucky day when she came into his life. She'd torn down his defenses, leaving him open and vulnerable, and he was falling hard for her. Nothing felt more right.

He strode to her bedroom door and knocked. "Cade?"

"It's me," he said, walking into the room. He grabbed her hand and lifted her up from her seat at the secretary desk. "Close your eyes."

"Why?"

"Just close them and come with me."

He covered her eyes with his hands, just to be sure. They penguin walked out of the room with him behind her until they reached the table by the fireplace set for two. "Okay, open them."

He stepped to her side to gauge her reaction. She opened her eyes and peered at the table, the fireplace, the candles, and her loving expression told him all he needed to know. "Oh, Cade. This is beautiful."

"Like you," he said, kissing her cheek.

"I love it."

"Well, I hope you like the food as much as this."

"It smells wonderful."

"Have a seat," he said. "I'll plate up the meal."

She smiled. "You're using all the right lingo."

"I should. I've been through three digital cookbooks today."

She laughed and then took her seat on the pillow.

He strode into the kitchen, his chest puffed out a

little. He'd made a good impression with the table setting—now he only hoped the meal was edible.

The riced potatoes looked good. They were a breeze. All it took to rice them was a strong arm and some herbs and butter. It was amazing how much different they tasted than regular old mashed potatoes. He laid those down on the plate first, then arranged two of the braised short ribs on top. He crisscrossed the asparagus on a slant, so that the stalks towered above the meat on an angle. For an amateur, it wasn't half-bad.

He brought the dishes to the table, serving Dawn first. She was staring at the fire, watching the embers burn. "Here you go."

She turned a discerning eye on the food, and her expression changed. "Cade. Wow."

"You haven't tasted it yet."

"I don't have to. I can see you did this perfectly. The presentation is half the battle. I know it's gonna be delish."

He rubbed the back of his neck. "Hope so."

Feeling accomplished, he took a seat. He hadn't been this content since before Bree. He sighed and waited for Dawn to take the first bite.

She managed to get a little portion of each dish onto her fork and then brought it to her mouth. She closed her eyes as she chewed, as if she could discern the different flavors that way. "Oh, yum."

"Really?"

"It's good, Cade. Really, really good."

He grinned. "Thanks."

She gazed at him, pride beaming from her eyes. "You did a great job on the meal."

"You didn't taste the biscuits yet. They didn't rise like I hoped."

She looked over at the basket on the table. The biscuits were flat and crunchy. "Making perfect biscuits is an art. I'll still eat them."

"You don't have to."

She grabbed one from the basket and chomped on it. She chewed and chewed. "Not bad for a first time."

"You're just trying to make me feel better."

"No, I'm not." She gave him an adorable wink. "I'm saving that for later, in the bedroom."

"Well in that case, I'll make you dinner every night."

She smiled as he poured wine, and then she raised her glass. "To you," she said, giving his glass a clink. "And your new cooking skills."

He went along with that, but secretly he toasted Dawn coming into his life, saving him from sinking into the quicksand of grief.

Cade sat on the bed, glancing down at Dawn. He didn't think he'd ever seen a more beautiful sight than the brunette lying there, her hair tousled, her expression so serene. She opened her eyes and immediately reached for him, wrapping her arms around his neck. "Mornin'," he said, bending to give her a kiss.

"Hmm." She sighed. "Why are you getting up so early?"

"Babe, it's not early. It's ten o'clock already."

They'd had quite a workout in bed last night. Just thinking about it made his body tighten and his pulse race.

"Ten o'clock?" Dawn popped up, the sheets covering her delicious body falling off her. "Why didn't you wake me?"

"Because you looked like Sleeping Beauty. Snored a bit, too."

"Cade, you know I don't snore."

"If you say so."

She tossed a pillow at him, and he went down laughing.

She laughed, too, as she scrambled off the bed. He reached for her, but she was too fast; she wiggled right out of his arms. "Oh no, you don't. We're late. I still have to put together lunch and we haven't even had coffee yet."

He gestured with his arms. "Look around and show me who cares?"

"I care. I'm being paid to feed you. And we've planned that trip around the lake. We were supposed to get an early start, remember?"

"Yes, but that was before we tripped all around the bed last night, remember?"

"So, you don't want to go?"

The disappointment in her voice tortured him. That, and the fact that she was buck naked in front of him, her lips in a pout. He'd rather spend the day in bed with her, but he wouldn't go back on his word. "Of course I want to go. We're not on any time schedule. Why don't you get ready and I'll meet you in the kitchen? I'll make coffee."

She smiled, a big, wide grin that warmed his heart. "Okay. I'll only be a few minutes."

"Oh, and wear those denim shorts—you know, the ones that are all torn up."

"You mean my Daisy Dukes?"

He swallowed hard. "Yeah, those."

She blew him a kiss. "I sure will."

He laughed and walked into the kitchen, shaking his head. He was in deep with Dawn, and it was the best place to be. She lightened his mood and made everything fun. Somehow, after all this was over, he'd find a way for them to be together.

He set coffee brewing. As he reached into the cabinet, bringing down two mugs, he heard a car pull up on the drive, and he frowned slightly in confusion. Who could that be? He walked over to the window and found three more cars pulling up behind the first one. Then a Channel 10 news van pulled up. "Oh, crap."

He knew what this was about. He wasn't gonna let these guys intrude on his vacation.

He opened the front door and walked out onto the porch. Cameras snapped his picture, and questions were immediately slung at him. He held up a hand, gesturing to stop, and leveled them all a hard look. "Not a step farther," he said, standing his ground at the foot of the porch. If he allowed them, they'd be shoving their microphones in his face.

What on earth did his brother, Gage, do now to

warrant the paparazzi seeking him out for a comment? Hell, he'd been down this road before, too many times.

"Where's Harper?" one reporter asked.

"Are you hiding out together?" another one shouted.

"Do you know the entire country is looking for Harper?" The questions were hurled at him, one right after the other.

"Who the hell is Harper?" he replied. "I think you've got the wrong guy here."

"Harper Dawn," a reporter shouted. "The woman you're living with."

"What?"

Just then, the door creaked open, and Dawn exited. "Go back inside," he told her. "This isn't about you."

Dawn didn't heed his warning, but instead stepped up next to him. Color drained from her face, her expression dire. She put a hand on his arm. "It is about me, I'm afraid. Cade, I'm so sorry."

"Sorry?" He blinked and blinked again. What was she talking about?

But at her appearance on the porch, the entire crowd started shouting questions at Dawn. His mind muddied up. What was happening? The reporters kept calling her Harper. Harper Dawn.

"When did you dye your hair?"

"Is it for your disguise?"

"Does this mean you don't love Dale Murphy anymore?"

"Yes, I'd like the answer to that myself." A man walked up, slender with blond hair and deceptively cool blue eyes. As if he were a god, the sea of paparazzi separated to let the guy through.

It was like a freak show gone bad, and Cade was right in the middle of it.

Harper silently prayed for guidance. The reporters were relentless. And Dale? Now, that was a surprise. Where had he come from? Why was he here looking forlorn? Her heart pounded hard against her chest.

She turned to Cade. He was…oh dear God, he stared at her with a mixture of confusion and panic. As if he was hoping for all of this to be some giant mistake that she could explain away. "Dawn?"

She squeezed her eyes shut briefly, shaking her head. "I'm so sorry, Cade. My name's not Dawn. Well, it is, but I'm Harper Dawn. And I was going to tell you—"

"It's true, then? You're not who you say you are? You're in some sort of disguise?"

She swallowed hard, tears forming in her eyes, but she refused to let the cameras catch her crying.

"She's Harper Dawn," the blond man said, "and I'm here to win her back. To remind her of our dream. We had beautiful plans to open a restaurant together. To be married, partners in love and life. I want you to be my one last date."

All the cameras turned toward Chef Dale, catching his plea. He stood there, bold but sympathetic in the eyes of the world. He was good, she'd give him that. He always knew how to capture the spotlight. She didn't love him. She never really had, but his charm and wit had had her fooled for a time. That's where she'd gone wrong.

The man she loved was standing beside her, and with each passing second his expression grew more and more grim. Cade was looking at her now like she was a monster. An ugly, lying, two-faced creature that disgusted him.

"One Last Date?" Cade's mouth twisted. "That reality show?" He looked out at the reporters, the news vans, now three in number, and she could see it in his expression as the full impact of her deceit hit him hard.

"That's right," Dale said. "We met on the show, and we fell in love."

"I didn't," she said to Cade, shaking her head adamantly. "I didn't love him."

Cade dismissed her denial. "You're a damn reality star?"

She shook her head. "No, no. It's not like that."

"She got cold feet is all," Dale said, "and ran off. But I'm not giving up on you, Harper. I'm here to ask for another chance."

Cade flinched and then gave her a look filled with pain and anger. Then his eyes narrowed, zeroing in on her. "Harper? My sister has a friend named Harper… do you know Lily?"

Oh crap. "I think we should go inside and talk, Cade."

"And deprive these vultures of a story?"

"Cade, please." She pleaded with him with everything she had inside. Her eyes burned from holding back tears. "Please."

He looked her up and down, battling with his decision, then jerked his head toward the door. "Get inside, *Harper.*"

She flinched. Oh man, this was a mess. "Are you c-coming?"

"It's my cabin."

She walked inside first, Cade directly behind her. He slammed the door shut and locked it. She was trembling, her legs weak. She had trouble breathing, her heart was racing so fast. Cade hated her. She could see it in his eyes. At least he hadn't left her out there—he hadn't tossed her to the wolves. They were still outside, shouting questions.

Cade walked straight to the liquor cabinet and poured himself a scotch. He downed it in one gulp, then poured himself another.

"Cade, please. Let me explain."

He glared at her from across the room, desolation in his eyes. She'd hurt him. She'd destroyed his trust and anything that they may have had. *Oh God.*

"Sit down," he ordered.

She took a seat on the sofa adjacent to the fireplace. The same one where they'd played rummy so many times, the same place where Cade had served her his first home-cooked meal.

He stood for a while, pacing. Not saying anything. Just gulping scotch and, apparently, trying to calm himself down.

When he finished the glass, he poured another, then took a seat. "Explain."

She began at the beginning, telling him how she and Lily had become friends. And how she'd been dating, wanting so badly to fall in love and be married. She wanted a family before she was thirty. She had a life plan that included opening a restaurant, and so when Chef Dale Murphy had been picked for *One Last Date*, Lily convinced her that she should join the show. Harper had deep reservations about it, but the producers loved the idea of putting another chef on, so before she knew it, she was chosen to be one of twelve women vying for love.

All the while she was explaining, Cade stared at the fireplace, refusing to look at her. His face was hard, and nothing she had to say seemed to change that.

"So, after I refused Dale's marriage proposal, I became public enemy number one. The press was horrid to me, hounding me everywhere I went. They knew where I lived, where my parents lived. I had nowhere else to go. So Lily offered to let me stay here at the cabin."

"Nice of my sister," he muttered sarcastically.

"It turned out you were coming here, too. They knew if you were told I was coming up here, you'd have an excuse to stay home and work. I didn't want to do it, Cade. But I was in a bind. And so Lily came up with the idea of me being your personal chef. It seemed harmless enough at the time. That way, both of us could stay here."

Cade rose from the sofa, looking down at her. "You got paid to sleep with me."

"No! I wasn't paid a thing." She lifted from the sofa to face him, hating that he'd jumped to such a conclusion. Hating that he thought that little of her. "I'm sorry, Cade. Really, really sorry. But I think you know, us being together intimately wasn't in the plan. It just happened." And it had been earth-shattering.

"For all I know, you were in on this from the beginning. Did the creators of the show get to you? Is that what this was all about? You did it for the ratings? Because honestly, I can't figure out what kind of woman has to go on a damn reality show to find love. Certainly, not one for me."

That stung, and she bit her lower lip, holding back tears. "Cade, that's not true."

"You lied to me over and over. About *everything*."

"I was going to tell you the truth. Honest, I was."

"I don't believe that," he said, his voice a deep growl. "I'll *never* believe that. You made a fool out of me, Harper. I feel like such an idiot. But you did show me a good time. You sure know your way around the bedroom."

She jerked back and gasped. She wanted to slap his face. He was being intentionally cruel. Maybe she deserved his wrath for bringing all this down on him, but she'd never thought Cade could be so hurtful. He tossed his tumbler into the fireplace. The sound of shattering glass echoed in the silence of the room, seeming to seal their fate. "I'm leaving," he said. "Stay or go, it's up to you."

As in, he didn't give a crap about what happened to her. "I'm...leaving, too."

From now on, she'd have to battle the paparazzi, but it would be a whole lot easier than trying to convince Cade she'd never meant to hurt him.

Seven

"I'm not leaving here until you speak to me." Lily stood in front of Cade's office desk at Tremaine Corp., tilting her chin at him stubbornly. His sister was the last person he wanted to see today. Well, make that the second-to-last person he wanted to see. His day had gone from bad to worse, and Lily was just the topping on the cake.

He rubbed the back of his neck and leaned back in his chair, staring up at her. "What is it this time?"

"You're working yourself to death, Cade. You're never home, and Mom's worried about you."

"I'm fine. Just busy doing what I love to do."

"You're not supposed to be working these long hours. You're under too much stress."

"Not as much stress as my last vacation," he shot back. "Remember, when you and Mom set me up?"

"We didn't set you up, brother. And if you'd stop feeling sorry for yourself long enough, you'll realize it. How many times do I have to apologize?"

"The best thing you can do for me is let it go."

"Cade, please."

He rose from his desk, his temper flaring. "No, Lily. Not this time. Have you seen the newspapers lately? My picture is splashed across the front page, with Chef Dale and Harper, or whatever her name is. I just love seeing my picture in the tabloids in a love-triangle-gone-bad headline. Geesh, Gage must be laughing his head off. He's usually the one on the front page." He looked out his office window and sighed. "How do you suppose that affects my blood pressure?"

"It's only been a few weeks. It'll die down soon."

He turned to face her. "A few weeks too many."

Every time he thought about *Harper*—he still thought of her as Dawn—his stomach knotted up. He didn't want to remember the good times. He certainly tried not thinking about how pretty she was, how sweet her body felt crushed up against his, how she moaned his name when he made love to her. He fought those thoughts on a daily basis, having only the reminder of her grand deceit to sway him back to reality. To the truth of her betrayal.

"Cade, Harper is terribly sorry. She's living with her folks now, barely holding on. She's not working. She's trying to keep a low profile. These past few weeks haven't been easy on her. The media won't leave her alone. She doesn't have security guards to keep them away, the way you do."

Cade hated hearing it. He hated that her folks were being hassled, too. It wasn't fair. They were innocent in all this. "I'll send some security to help out. For her parents' sake."

"Just for her parents?"

"Yeah, Lil. Don't read anything else into it."

"I've already offered, but Harper won't hear of it. She refused help."

"Then that's that." So why was his gut twisting? Why was he feeling like crap all of a sudden?

"Is there anything else?" he asked Lily. He wanted her to leave so he could put these feelings aside and dive back into his work.

"Yes, now that you asked." Lily plopped down on the leather seat facing his desk. "Sit down. We need to talk about Mom's seventieth birthday."

"What about it?"

"It's happening in less than a month. We have to make arrangements. I need your input."

He took a seat and shook his head. "You don't need me. You can do this."

"You expect me to plan a party for 150 people on my own? No way, bro. That's a big undertaking. Gage is flying in special the day before her birthday, so that leaves you and me."

"Hire a company or party planner or whatever to do it."

"Not gonna happen. Mom wouldn't appreciate it

as much, and you know it. We need to make this special for her."

"Okay, fine. I'll help. But today's a killer."

"How about on Saturday morning?"

"Fine, we'll talk on Saturday."

"Great." Lily gave him a big smile. "I'll see you Saturday. And Cade, just so you know, Harper is doing about as well as you are right now."

"Go," he commanded, pointing to the door. Lily bounced out of the office with pep in her step. What on earth was she so happy about all the time?

He went back to work, looking blankly at his computer screen, Lily's last words echoing in his ears. *Harper is doing about as well as you are right now.*

He'd fallen for her, and she'd made a fool out of him. He shouldn't feel anything but contempt for her. Yet knowing that she was hurting, too, didn't make him feel any better.

It just made his day even more horrible.

"That's a sweet girl," Harper said as she stroked Queenie's pure white fur. The cat sat on her lap purring, her little motor running full speed. "It's been a long time since you've gotten this much love from me, hasn't it?" she asked softly, running her hands over the cat's back, sinking her fingers into her fur and then rubbing her behind the ears. Every so often she'd stop petting her and the cat would turn to look her in the eye, as if to say, *do more.*

Why not? She didn't have anything else to do. She hadn't left her parents' house since she'd gotten here two weeks ago, and now only an occasional news van would show up in front of the house. Lucky for her, her father was a survivalist. They had enough food and supplies for months, and her parents had hunkered down with her, lying low. They claimed they were glad to stay at home and not give the press what they wanted. She loved them for trying to protect her, but it was a great inconvenience to them.

Her mom made sure to give her extra hugs every day, and her dad would give her a good-night kiss before turning in. Just like when she was a little girl. They were the best, and she hated putting them in this position. That's why she'd gone up to the cabin—to avoid causing them this grief. Not to mention the embarrassment of the scandal she'd created. A love triangle, the tabloids had said, with her right smack in the middle of it.

She didn't know if she'd ever get back to doing what she loved, to being a chef. Right now, she was known as a heartbreaker. Period.

"Honey, I brought you some hot tea."

Her mom's cure for whatever ails you was always herbal tea. She didn't have the heart to tell her mom she preferred coffee.

"It's raspberry hibiscus."

"Sounds yummy. Thanks, Mom."

Her mother set two teacups down on the cocktail table and took a seat on the sofa next to her. Queenie hadn't moved a muscle, and her mother gave the cat a loving scratch under the chin. "She really is a queen," Harper said.

"We've spoiled her."

"The same way you've spoiled me."

"Oh, honey, we're not spoiling you, we're support- ing you and letting you know we have your back. Dad and I hate to see you so sad."

"I'm not *that* sad, Mom. Just at loose ends."

Her mom reached for her hand. "I know it seems hopeless right now. But this will pass. You just have to be patient."

"I've worked so hard to make a name for myself. I have a publisher interested in my cookbook, but I haven't had the heart to work on it for weeks now. I gave up my job to go on *One Last Date* and now, just because I couldn't go through with a marriage proposal, no one will hire me because suddenly I'm this big villain."

"Not to everyone."

"I appreciate your support, Mom."

"That's not what I mean. Have you looked on so- cial media?"

"Social media? Mom, what do you know about that?"

"Hey, your mom wasn't born in the stone ages. I know about those sites. I've been reading some of those posts, and there's more than a few people who are on your side. They say you stuck up for your prin- ciples and decided to follow what your brain and your heart were telling you to do."

"Really?"

"Yes, really. So not everyone's against you. And

for those trolls who are bashing you, I say, so what? They don't define you. *You* define you."

Harper sipped her tea. Her mother was amazing, giving her this pep talk and making her see things from an entirely different perspective. It gave her a mental boost. "Thanks, Mom. That means a lot to me."

Her mother gave her hand a squeeze. "That's my girl. You need to get back out there. You need to show them that you're not going to let them hold you back."

Her cell phone rang, and she looked at the screen. "It's Lily," she told her mom.

"I'll let you girls talk," her mom said, rising from the sofa.

"Mom, I can call her back. We haven't finished our tea."

"No, no. It's fine, sweetheart. You can talk to me anytime. You talk to Lily and tell her I said hello."

"Okay, Mom. Thanks." She sat up straighter and answered the phone. "Hi, Lily."

"Hi, you."

It was great to hear Lily's voice. They spoke every other day, keeping in touch with each other without mentioning the sore subject of Cade. "How's your day going?"

"Okay, I guess. I'm knee-deep in preparations for my mother's birthday. It's a big challenge. I don't know how party planners do it."

"Some might say the same about interior decorators. All those choices, but you manage to put together amazing looks. I guess it's all about your passion."

"I guess so."

"Speaking of passion, any luck on getting a position?"

"No one's beating down my door for my culinary talents, I can tell you that. I miss working."

"Are the sleaze buckets still out there?"

"Actually, it's been much better. They're not camped out in front of the house anymore. I've yet to go outside, though, afraid someone will be lurking around a corner."

"That's no way to live."

"Tell me about it."

"Well, I have a solution to your problem, but I want you to hear me out before you say anything. Promise?"

"The last time I promised you something, I wound up on a reality show."

"I know, but this is different. It'll be good for your career."

Harper took a steadying breath. After her mother's pep talk, she had a newfound desire to get back to her old life. Where she was respected as a chef, and as a person. Where she could walk down the street holding her head high.

"I'm listening, Lil."

"Remember to let me speak. As you know, I've been working on my mother's birthday bash and I've been going full steam ahead, but I ran into a roadblock, and it's something you can possibly help me with."

"Me? What can I do to help?"

"Well, you see, Mom's very fussy about certain things, and dining is very important to her. Her favorite caterer needed emergency surgery yesterday and she had to cancel on us. It's not her fault or anything, but now, with such short notice, we're sort of stuck. I was thinking, hoping, that you could take her place as our chef. Of course, we'd pay you, and you'd have a team to help you. So, um, I know it's a lot to ask, but you've been wanting to get back to work, and this is a really good gig. Would you consider doing it?"

"I assume Cade will be there?"

"Of course. It's our mother's seventieth birthday."

"Then no. I can't help you. Sorry, Lil."

"Wait a minute, you haven't even thought about it."

"I don't need to think about it. Look, I appreciate you thinking of me, but there's no way I'm going to impose myself on your family and cause any more trouble. You and I both know Cade doesn't want me there."

She heard Lily sigh on the other end of the phone. "And I also know you're in love with him."

"So?"

"So, are you giving up so easily? You must not love him enough to fight for him. But if it was as amazing being with him as you said, then I'd say he was worth one more try. He's a good guy and you brought him out of his heartache, Harper. You ended his grieving, and that's really something."

"He hates me, Lily."

"You know what they say. There's a fine line between love and hate."

"That's a cliché and doesn't pertain to me."

"Still, clichés exist for a reason. And I say it does pertain to you. It's a chance to take on a challenge, both in the kitchen and out. We have two weeks to prep. One hundred fifty guests to feed and you'll have to be here to set up the menu with my mother, to train your team. We've got a cozy guesthouse on the property you can stay at while you prep. And you'll be making a name for yourself as an accomplished chef. Doesn't that sound perfect?"

"It would be if…"

"If what?"

"I'll do it only if Cade agrees. I'm not going to spring this on him. Everything has to be cleared by Cade or I won't come."

"I'll talk to him," Lily said.

"No, Lily, I'll speak with him. That's if he'll get on the phone with me. After all, I'm the one who got in this mess, so it's up to me to make things right. Or as right as they can be, under the circumstances."

"Okay, I think that's fair. You've got the job, if Cade agrees."

"Thanks, Lily." She hung up the phone and closed her eyes. If she was going to do this, it had to be now. Otherwise, she might just chicken out.

She immediately texted Cade. Hi Cade, it's Harper. I'd like to speak with you on the phone. Is it okay for me to call you? Please.

Now the ball was in his court. All she had to do was wait for him to reply.

Or not.

* * *

Cade sat in the game room in his favorite suede chair, fully focused on the television screen as he sipped bourbon straight up. *One Last Date* was an idiot concept, and he'd often wondered about the people who actually went on that show. Granted, he'd never once tuned in before, and he was surprised at the occupations of the contestants. There were attorneys, nurses, stockbrokers and *chefs*.

He sat mesmerized watching the women—well, one woman—in her quest for love. Pretty curly-blond-haired Harper Dawn seemed to be the fan favorite, and he could hardly believe she was the same woman he'd spent time with at Bright Landing. The transformation blew his mind, and it had taken him a few episodes to actually believe that Dawn didn't exist—never existed. Harper was a completely different woman. She had paired up nicely with Chef Dale Murphy. Both shared a love of food, cooking and entertaining. They looked good together.

Cade fast-forwarded their kissing scenes, barely able to watch further. But he persisted as Harper looked straight into the camera, giving her testimonial about what she wanted in a man. About her feelings for Dale. But there was something missing in her speech. And as Cade continued watching episode after episode, he began to notice little things about Dale Murphy, culinary chef. He spoke to Harper constantly about opening a restaurant together, about how they made a good team, but on their cooking dates, Dale would question Harper's judgment and give her backhanded compliments. It was apparent he was trying to make himself look the more competent chef by his subtle innuendo.

The more Cade saw, the more he thought the guy an egotistical jerk.

"Cade, are you in here?" His mother, Rose, walked into the room, and he immediately paused the show.

"Yep, I'm in here."

He sipped his drink and looked up at her, caught in the act.

"Bingeing on something?" she asked, taking the seat next to him.

It was obvious he was. "Just trying to keep up on the times."

"By watching *One Last Date*?"

"It's must-see television."

"You're watching Harper, trying to make sense of all this."

"Mom, what kind of woman goes on a reality dating show to find love?"

"Someone who's ready for love, I suppose."

He shook his head. "I don't get it. Dawn—I mean, Harper—was a different person than I'm seeing here. I'm not sure which one she is. I don't know her at all. And the lies she told, the whole deception, I'm sorry, but I can't help but compare her to Bree. Bree never would've done anything like that to me. Heck, not even Madeline would've done something like this." Madeline was an old girlfriend, someone he'd dated for an entire year before he met Bree.

His mother took his hand. "Cade, in your mind

Bree was perfect. She was a saint compared to other women, but she was rare. Not everyone can be that perfect. You shouldn't measure all women against Bree's memory. People make mistakes, especially when they're backed into a corner. And I hate to see you give up on someone you obviously care about because of her mistakes. And mine. And Lily's. Try to remember that as you finish watching these episodes. Keep an open mind, son. You don't want to shoot yourself in the foot."

"Dad would say that." He smiled.

"And where do you think he got it from?" His mom squeezed his hand and rose from the seat. "Love you, Cade."

He nodded, his heart warming. "Love you, too, Mom."

And an hour later, he was still watching the show, having reached episode seven, when his cell phone buzzed. He glanced at the screen. It was Harper. His eye began to twitch. He never thought she'd contact him. He had mixed feelings about reading the text, but his curiosity got the better of him. He opened the text, scanning it quickly. She asked if she could speak with him, if she could call him. He wrote back. It's late. Maybe tomorrow. His finger was on the send button, and he stared at his curt reply. No sense being a jerk about it. He erased it and wrote instead, We can talk tomorrow, okay?

She returned the message immediately. Okay, thanks!

Cade's gut clenched. He had no idea what she

wanted, and that put him on edge. Maybe he shouldn't have been so quick to agree. Did he really want to speak with Harper? He wasn't sure. She was all he would think about when he let down his guard.

Folding his arms across his chest, he hunkered down into the cushions of the chair, determined to watch *One Last Date* to the bitter end. He didn't think he'd get much sleep tonight, anyway. Not with thoughts of Harper Dawn invading his head.

"Honey, it's good to see you cooking again. Are you experimenting with a new dish for your cookbook?"

"I am, Mom." Harper was at the stove, putting together an egg-white scramble, a healthy alternative for breakfast. "I've decided to take hold of my life again. What do you think of *Healthy and Hearty with Harper* for the title of my cookbook?"

"I think it's wonderful."

"It's pretty catchy, right? I'm going to dedicate it to you and Dad if the publisher offers me a contract." So far, she'd only gotten offers to do a tell-all book about her time on *One Last Date*. That was so not happening.

"That's sweet, honey. Your dad and I will be honored. And it's not *if*, but when it gets published."

"You have such faith in me. I wish I felt that confident."

"Give yourself some time. This whole ordeal has you rattled. But I think it'll work out in the long run. You're talented, Harper."

"Thanks, Mom. Love you."

"Love you right back."

An hour later, Harper paced back and forth in her bedroom. Her mother had kept her room pretty much intact from when she lived here. She loved the warmth and coziness that still remained, the thick lavender comforter, the pillows in the shape of hearts, the posters of a younger Tim McGraw and Rascal Flatts on the walls. Whenever she came to visit, it was always a comfort to sleep in her old room.

She glanced out the window. The time for stalling was over. She needed to call Cade, and her future could very well be in the balance. She dialed his phone number and waited. It rang, two, three, four times, and just when she thought it was going to voice mail, he picked up. "Hello."

"Hi, it's me," she said.

"Which me is it?" he asked.

Oh boy, he wasn't going to make this easy.

"It's Harper. The same person you know, except by a different name."

"I doubt that, but go on."

She counted to three before answering. At least he hadn't hung up on her. That was encouraging. What wasn't encouraging was the way her heart pounded and her stomach churned just hearing his deep, masculine voice. It did things to her. Reminded her of happier times.

"How are you, Cade?"

"Fine. Perfect."

He didn't ask how she was, and that should tell her

something. "I, uh, that's good to hear. Are you busy? Because I can call you later if you are."

"Harper." He always seemed to say her name with contempt, or was she reading too much into it? "Say what you have to say."

"Okay, well, you know how sorry I am about the way things turned out. And I don't suppose you want to see me and I'm not asking for that. But what I am asking for is a chance to help out your family and try to get my reputation back as a chef. Right now, because of the scandal, I haven't been working. I, uh, quit my job to go on the show, and I'm not sure restaurants are going to hire a chef that comes with so much controversy. And, well, since Lily is in a bind to find someone to prepare your mom's birthday meal, she asked me to do it. But," she rushed out, "I will only take the job if it's okay with you. I mean, you wouldn't have to see me. I promise to steer clear of you. I'll be working hard prepping the meals and training the crew. I told Lily it all depends on what you say."

"So, let me get this right. You're asking my permission to come here as a chef and work my mother's birthday bash."

"Yes, that's right."

She heard him sigh into the phone. There was a long pause. "I'm not sure it's a good idea."

Tears welled in her eyes, not from losing the job, but because Cade hated her so much he really wanted nothing more to do with her. "I…understand. Well, then there's not much else to—"

"I'm not sure it's a good idea, but yeah. I won't stand in your way if you want the job."

"So, I have your blessing?"

"Hardly that. But Mom needs a chef and you need the work."

"I'll take that." Her spirits lifted. "Thank you, Cade."

He remained quiet, and she decided to end the call before he changed his mind.

"Bye, Cade." Gently, she hung up the phone and fist-pumped the air several times before flopping on her bed with a big grin.

She was going to make the Tremaine party the best they'd ever had.

Even if she'd have to tiptoe around Cade the whole time she was there.

Eight

"I'm so glad you're here," Lily said, giving Harper a big, squeezy kind of hug. Her friend's arms felt good around her. Harper needed to know one person was happy she was here. But she couldn't think about Cade right now. She had one week to pull this all together.

"Lily, you're such a great friend. I needed that kind of welcome."

"You're an equally good friend, and you look good."

Harper rolled her eyes. "I don't, but thanks for saying that." She looked out at the view of the estate from the steps of the guesthouse. "Wow, your home is amazing. I've seen pictures of it, but they don't do it justice."

"I can't believe you've never been here before. Seems weird."

"I know. I guess the timing was never right for me to visit."

"Yeah, I remember how busy we both were back then. But you're here now, and I can't wait to show you around. But first things first. Here's the key to the house." Lily handed it to her.

She glanced down at the key. "What's also weird is you're always handing me keys to your family's homes."

"Nothing weird about that."

Lily was always upbeat. It was hard not to be happy around her. Hard, but not impossible. Right now she was somewhere between nervous and excited.

"Come on, let's go inside."

As they stepped into the house, the vibe Harper got was nothing short of perfect. It was a spacious guesthouse with a Southwestern flair, lots of windows, tall ceilings and a rock fireplace. She walked into the kitchen and smiled. It was well stocked, with long granite countertops and all the appliances, big and small, a chef would ever need. "Nice kitchen."

"If you think this is nice, wait until you see the kitchen in the main house. It's state-of-the-art."

"Now you've got me really excited."

"Let's take your luggage to your room." She grabbed one bag as Harper grabbed the other and they moved down the hallway. "Take a peek and pick whichever room you like."

Both were pretty. One was in a neutral tone, with

furnishings that would suit either a male or female guest, and the other was done in warm melon and cream tones. It was an easy choice. "I like this one."

"Yep, that's my favorite, too," Lily said.

She was suddenly overwhelmed with gratitude. "Thanks for all this, Lil. And for picking me up today at my apartment. You didn't have to go so far out of your way."

"I wanted to. Just in case any stray photographers dogged you."

"Luckily, I think they've moved on. At least I hope they have ever since Dale said he's given up on the two of us. I think he just wanted the sympathetic press to help him launch his new restaurant."

"That sleaze."

"I don't blame him. I think he was convinced we would be perfect together. But unfortunately, I realized the only sparks we generated was when we were cooking in the kitchen. That was it. There was nothing real between us romantically."

"You made the right decision, hon."

"At least I did one thing right." She smiled. She was not going to be Debbie Downer this week and ruin Lily's mood.

"Well, enough talk about the past. Why don't you settle in, and I'll come get you, say, in two hours. We'll have a meeting with Mom and nail down the menu. She's anxious to see you."

"Gosh, it'll be good to see her, too."

"Sounds good."

Lily gave her a kiss on the cheek. "Welcome to our home, Harper."

"Thanks, Lil."

After Lily left, Harper unpacked her bags and put her toiletries in the bathroom. She thought she was too keyed up to rest, but suddenly a bout of fatigue hit her. She took off her clothes, put on an oversize T-shirt and set her phone alarm to wake her in forty-five minutes. That should give her plenty of time to dress before meeting Rose. She lay down on the comfy queen bed and closed her eyes, managing to shove aside all of her doubts and fears about this job and this place and simply let her mind clear.

A few raps on the front door woke her from her nap. She glanced at the time on her phone—Lily was really early. "Coming," she called out. "I'll be right there."

She padded to the front door and opened it. "Sorry, I thought you said two hours—"

But she didn't finish her thought, because it wasn't Lily who stood on her doorstep.

It was Cade.

"Oh, uh..." For a few seconds they just stared into each other's eyes. Then Cade's gaze lifted to her honey-blond hair—now back to its natural color—and the waves that swept over her shoulders. Next, he moved down to her chest, reading the words on her T-shirt: Chefs Like It Hot. His brow lifted at that and then his gaze traveled farther down to her exposed thighs. He took all of her in, his expression unreadable but for a certain gleam in his eyes.

"You look…"

Her heart pounding, her hand automatically touched the tips of her hair. "Different, I know."

But he looked different, too. He was wearing a white dress shirt tucked into a pair of slacks—business clothes. So different from the guy who wore jeans and T-shirts all day long back at the cabin. Although, with the sleeves rolled up and his collar open, he was just as drop-dead gorgeous and sexy.

He nodded, his lips tight as if he was remembering her disguise, her lies.

"What are you doing here? I mean, you have every right to be here, since this is your house, but I never expected you to—"

"I thought it would be less weird if we saw each other in person privately first, rather than giving the family a show if we bumped into each other in front of them."

She nibbled on her lower lip. For a second there, she'd had hope. "I see… It's weird now, too."

"At least we don't have an audience."

Because he would hate that. She was grateful that he didn't mention *One Last Date* and that audience.

"I'm sorry, Cade."

"I didn't come here for an apology. I know you're sorry."

Well, that was to the point. "Would you like to come in?"

He swept his gaze over her body once again, quickly this time, and he shook his head. "No."

But his eyes said something different. His eyes

gave him away. He didn't trust her. She knew that. But he seemed to be struggling, trying to remain distant.

"Is there anything else?"

"Not really, no. Just wanted to break the ice."

"Consider it broken," she said softly. "And thanks again for agreeing to let me do this. It means a lot."

He gave her another nod. "Anything for Mom's birthday."

The meaning wasn't lost on her. He'd do anything for his mom, including enduring Harper's presence at the estate for an entire week.

"Goodbye, Cade." She shut the door, but his arm came out immediately to stop her.

"Wait." He sighed and shook his head. "That came out wrong."

"Did it?"

"It honestly did. I'm not here to hurt you."

"It's okay, Cade. I've got to get dressed. I've got a meeting with your mom in a few minutes. So, if you're through, I'd better be going."

He let go of the door. "Yeah, sure."

She closed it slowly and heard Cade curse under his breath as he walked away. "That went well," she muttered before slumping against the door, trying to hold back tears.

The Tremaine kitchen was almost the size of a small house. There were three large workstations, long counters and two double ovens, not to mention the Sub-Zero refrigerators. Two sliding glass French doors led out to a wraparound patio shaded from the afternoon sun by an awning and a yard that would easily hold 150 people. A large stone fireplace sat in the corner of the patio, and the lawn furniture would be perfect for the guests to sit and have drinks and appetizers. She envisioned the scene in her head. It would be lovely when all was said and done.

"Hello, Harper."

The sound of Rose's gentle voice made her turn from the French doors. They'd met a few times and had had lunch once when she'd come to visit Lily at school and later at graduation. "Hi, Mrs. Tremaine."

"It's Rose, please. Thank you for coming on such short notice." She walked over to Harper and gave her a brief hug.

The gesture meant a lot. She'd take all the hugs she could get lately. "Of course, it's my pleasure."

"It's good to see you, Harper. You're looking well."

"Thank you." But Rose Tremaine looked like the epitome of Southern grace and style. Her silver-pearl hair flipped at the shoulders and shone brilliantly in the daylight. Her eyes were clear sky blue, and so pretty. "It's great to see you, too."

"Mom, Harper is all settled in at the guesthouse," Lily said.

"I hope you find it comfortable."

"It's very comfortable. And this house, especially this kitchen, is like a dream come true."

"Can I get you two anything?" Lily asked. "Some iced tea or lemonade? Or something stronger?"

"I'm fine," Harper said.

"Lily, why don't you bring a pitcher of iced tea

over with some glasses? And Irene made some fresh blueberry muffins this morning. Bring those, too."

"Sure, Mom."

"Irene is the family cook," Rose said. "She's been with us twenty years. She'll be around all week to help with the party."

"Great."

"But before we talk about the menu, I need to apologize to you about the mix-up at the cabin."

Heat rushed up Harper's throat, and her cheeks burned. She didn't want to talk about this. She was trying to put it all behind her. "There's no apology necessary, really."

"Lily and I put you in a bad spot. We realize that now."

"But you really helped me, too, since I had nowhere else to go. It was just an impossible situation. And, well, I never meant to hurt anyone."

"Cade's a big boy. He'll come around."

"He's not happy I'm here."

"I wouldn't be too sure of that, Harper. But my meddling days are over. Now, shall we talk about the menu? I was thinking surf and turf. But I'm open to all of your ideas, too."

"Sure, I'm thrilled to talk about my ideas." She opened the file folder she'd brought along. She had been writing down her notes ever since she accepted this job. "I have a list of five options for the meal plan. Or we can combine, as you fit."

"You're organized—I like that."

"I love what I do. It helps."

She and Lily and Rose stayed at the table until every detail of the menu, including appetizers, drinks and desserts, was nailed down. Rose handed her a list of caterers in the area, many of whom would be willing to work alongside her as sous chefs. She would be calling them later today. And though Harper could do desserts, she opted to bring in a pastry chef. Once all their business was conducted and Harper was satisfied, she rose from the table. "Thanks for your input," she said to Rose and Lily. She grabbed her folder filled with notes and tucked it under her arm. "I'm excited to get started on this. I'll be at the guesthouse, in case either of you think of something we missed."

"Oh, I think we've covered everything," Lily said.

"Dinner is at seven," Rose said.

"Oh, but I can't, uh…I'll be working into the night."

"Nonsense, Harper. You have to eat. And while you're here, you're our guest. We wouldn't dream of not having you for dinner."

"Yes, ma'am. But then there's the matter of…"

Lily took her hand. "Mom's right, Harp. There's no reason why you can't have dinner with us."

"That's right," came the masculine voice from behind her. She turned and faced Cade, who was standing in the kitchen doorway, looking handsome as always. "You should have dinner with the family. I won't be joining you."

The implication was clear. Cade was avoiding her, but he didn't have to be the one doing the avoiding. She'd promised she would steer clear of him. "I don't want to drive you off," she said quietly. "It's not what we agreed on."

"Harper, I have dinner plans of my own tonight."

"Oh, uh, I see." Was it the truth? Was he having dinner with a woman?

"Well, I've gotta get to the office. See you all later," he said.

Everyone said their farewells, and after he was gone, Harper exchanged glances with Rose and Lily. Both had sympathy in their eyes.

"Brothers," Lily mumbled.

Rose remained silent.

"I guess I'll see you in a few hours at dinner."

Lily and Rose both nodded.

Harper walked out of the kitchen, an ache in the pit of her stomach. At the very least, Cade was missing time with his family to avoid her. At the very worst, he had a dinner date with another woman.

"Irene, this meal was delicious," Harper told the Tremaine cook. She was a woman in her early fifties, a little bulky around the middle, with a pleasant smile and pale green eyes. "I ate up everything, and I usually don't do that."

"Coming from you, I'll take that as a compliment. Thank you, Chef Harper."

"It's just Harper, unless the sous chefs are around." She and Irene exchanged smiles. "Which, I'm happy to say, are all lined up. We'll have a staff of seven."

"That's wonderful," Rose said. "And yes, the salmon was delicious, Irene."

"It really was perfectly cooked. It's hard to get just right," Harper added.

Irene beamed. "Thank you. I'll bring coffee and dessert out now."

"Oh, none for me, thank you," Harper said. "I'm so full, I couldn't eat another bite."

"Are you sure?" Lily asked. "Irene makes a to-die-for caramel apple pie."

She patted her tummy. "I'm sure. Maybe I'll grab a bite tomorrow. Thanks for dinner, everyone. I think I'll turn in early tonight."

Lily walked her out, lacing their arms together like the true friend she was. "So, tell me. How was your first day here?"

"Actually, it went pretty smoothly. Better than I expected."

"That's good. You didn't seem to react to seeing Cade again."

"That's because he paid me a visit earlier today to break the ice. He didn't want to have an audience when we first saw each other again."

"Is that right? You didn't tell me."

"I'm telling you now."

"Hmm, he wasn't as shocked as I thought he'd be."

Lily drew her closer and whispered in her ear. "I think I know why."

"Why?"

"He's been watching *One Last Date*. Mom let it slip one day, but she wouldn't elaborate."

"Are you sure? I can't see Cade watching the

show. That's not something he would do. He thinks the whole idea is ridiculous."

"I'm only telling you what I know."

They'd reached the front door. "Whatever. I've got too much on my mind to think about it." She kissed Lily's cheek. "Thanks for being the best friend ever."

Lily took a bow. "That's me. Best friend extraordinaire."

They both giggled at her silliness, and then Harper walked out.

The night was cool, and she decided to take a walk around the premises, partly because she'd eaten too much and needed to exercise, and partly to clear her head about Cade. Of all the millions who'd watched *One Last Date*, he was the one person she'd hoped never would. Goodness, she'd revealed so much about herself on that show, exposing her feelings, which she usually held inside. Those producers had a knack for drawing out her deepest emotions. And when she'd rejected Dale when he was down on one knee, all hell had broken loose.

She closed her eyes, wondering when that memory would fade. The sound of horses snorting drew her gaze over to the stables, and she began heading in that direction. It wasn't far from the main house, but the moon had vanished behind the clouds, so she made her way under the guidance of ground lights, crossing the road.

A car came to a careening halt from behind, and she jumped back and turned. Headlights beamed in her face, and she squinted at the blinding light. Her heart pounded.

Someone jumped out of the car, slamming the door. "Geesh, Harper. Are you okay?"

She put her hand to her forehead to block the head-lights' glare. "C-cade?"

"Yeah, it's me." He walked over to within a foot of her and looked her over from head to toe. "You sure you're okay?"

She nodded. "I'm fine."

"I didn't see you. Damn it, I could've hit you." He ran a hand down his face. "What were you doing on the road all the way down here?"

"I, uh, was taking a walk and heard the horses."

The gravity of what almost happened finally dawned on her. She swayed back, and Cade caught her arms. He stared at her and his jaw tightened, his eyes in shadow as he gave her arms a gentle up-and-down rub before letting her go. His gentle caress, though brief, touched every part of her body.

"You wanted to see the horses?"

"Yes, I just needed a little more time before turning in."

"Hang on a second." He walked back to his car, a silver Beamer, and turned off the engine. Imme-diately the bright lights disappeared. "There, that's better," he said, coming to stand beside her. "Come on. Let's go."

"Go?" She shook her head, confused.

"I was heading to the stables. I like to check on my horses whenever I can."

She pointed in the opposite direction. "Maybe I should walk back to the guesthouse, let you go see the horses on your own."

Cade sighed heavily. "You want to see the horses. I want to see the horses. I think we can manage that."

"If you're sure. I'd love to see them."

"Follow me," he said, taking off and not giving her another chance to decline.

She caught up to him on the third stride, and together they headed toward the stables. "How many horses do you have?"

"The ranch has over twenty. We're breeding them. It's a small operation that our wrangler, Nathan Haines, heads up. I have three horses, Pepper, Cinnamon and Sage."

"I see a trend here. I like it."

"Bree named them," he said. "She didn't like power names. Said they were cliché."

"How so?"

"Well, Storm is big around here. So is Bolt or Thunder."

"I see what she meant. Is it hard talking about her?"

Cade's mouth twitched, but then he shook his head. "Not so much anymore." He gave her a look, one she couldn't quite grasp. "You helped me with that."

She swallowed a big lump in her throat. So, she was his rebound girl, who came before the one who would hold his heart for good.

They entered the stables, and they were magnificent. The facilities were clean, and it was obvious the horses were well taken care of in the large stalls. Somehow, she figured if Cade had anything to do with it, it wouldn't be any other way. She followed him to where his three horses were kept, and as soon as they spotted him, their ears perked up and they rushed to greet him, hanging their heads over the gate. He grabbed a bunch of carrots and handed Harper a couple. "Here, feed Sage. She's real gentle. Don't be afraid to show her some love. She eats it up."

"As long as she doesn't eat my hand."

He laughed, and the sound was beautiful to hear. "I'll get the other two."

She watched him feed and love up his mares, stroking them and speaking sweet words in their ears. It almost made her jealous, if one could be jealous of such regal animals. But she had no right to be jealous. She'd blown it with Cade, and though he was civil to her, that ship had sailed.

"You know, if you ever want to ride her, I'll let Nathan know. He could take you out one day."

"Oh, thanks. But that isn't happening. I have too much work to do for the party."

"Yeah, I heard you have a great menu planned."

"Thanks. It'll be a challenge."

"You'll do fine. Better than fine."

"That's nice of you to say."

"I wouldn't say it if I didn't mean it."

She smiled, and he blinked a few times. Tension mounted between them. She could feel it in the way he looked at her, the softness in his eyes, the way he'd touched her earlier. It was murder standing here, with him being nice to her like this.

She couldn't hope.

She wouldn't hope.

"I'd better get some sleep," she told him. "It's getting late."

"I'll drive you back."

"No, I feel like walking."

"I'll walk you back, then."

"Cade, why?" she implored him.

"Why what? Why do I want to see you safely back home? Maybe it's because I almost ran you down tonight. It sorta freaked me out. I can't lose anoth—"

"Cade, I can walk back by myself. Thanks, but I think it's best for us to keep our distance. This…this is hard for me, too."

She gave Sage one more pat on the head, turned and walked out of the stable. Hoping Cade wouldn't follow her.

His mother and Lily were sipping coffee in the kitchen when Cade came downstairs the next morning. They were the last people he wanted to see right now. They'd caused all this trouble, and now he was feeling the brunt of seeing Harper and wanting her when he should be keeping his distance. The irony was, he'd set the terms that they were to steer clear of each other, and he was the one wanting to break the rules.

For no other reason than he missed her.

She was all wrong for him, he knew that, but she

was like a magnet, pulling him toward her, and he couldn't seem to break free.

He turned to leave before his mom and sis spotted him. "Hey, Cade. Where're you going?" Lily asked. "Come have coffee with us."

"Yes," his mother said. "Irene made your breakfast. Don't let it get cold."

"I'm not hungry," he said, turning and walking over to the table. He slumped into the chair, put his elbows on the table and ran his hands through his hair.

"You look awful," Lily said. She was a master at saying the obvious. "Bedhead and bloodshot eyes."

"I didn't sleep much," he said.

Lily poured him a cup of coffee and placed it in front of him.

"Hope you're not coming down with something, Cade." His mother's face crinkled for a second, the way it would when he was a kid and had a fever.

"I think he is. I think it's called Harper syndrome."

He slanted his sister a look. "Very funny."

"I thought things with you two were running smoothly," his mother said. "I mean, my goodness, you've barely seen each other."

"Maybe he's seen her more than we know." Lily was prodding him, trying to pry information out of him.

"Lily, give it a rest. I almost ran her down last night with my car."

"What?" Mom and Lily both chorused in disbelief.

"How?" Lily asked.

"What happened, son?"

"I was coming home from my dinner with Madeline and her dad when—"

"You went out with *Madeline*?" Lily jumped in.

"Yes, and her dad, Martin O'Shea. It was business—my business and none of yours."

"If Madeline was there, it wasn't all business," Lily pronounced.

His sister could be a real pain in the ass sometimes. "Okay, whatever you say." He wasn't about to explain his relationship with his ex-girlfriend right now. Her dad and the Tremaines had been doing business together for over a decade now. Martin O'Shea owned a chain of hay and feed stores throughout the Southwest. Cade hadn't dated Madeline in over four years, though he was surprised to learn she wasn't seriously involved with anyone right now.

"Hush, Lily. Go on, Cade. Tell us about last night." His mom had had a way of breaking up would-be fights ever since he and his siblings could talk.

"Well, I was driving down our road, and it was black as pitch last night. I didn't expect anyone to step foot on the road without looking, and I slammed on my brakes just short of hitting Harper. God, talk about a deer-in-the-headlights look. On both our faces."

"Poor Harper. Is she okay?"

"I think so. She wouldn't let me drive her or walk her home."

"That's your doing, Cade." Lily rubbed salt into the wound.

Cade stared down at his coffee cup. "The thing

is…I might still…" He sighed then and shook his head. "I don't know."

Cade glanced at his mother. Sympathy filled her eyes. "I think it's best if you sort out your feelings. Before either of you gets hurt again."

"Harper's only obeying the rules you set down," Lily said. "Well, speak of the devil." His sister's eyes went to the kitchen doorway, and in walked Harper.

"Good morning," she said. "I hope it's okay—Irene let me in."

"Of course it's okay," his mother said, getting up. "Come have a seat. We have more than enough breakfast to go around."

"Oh no, thanks. I've already—"

Cade turned around in his seat to face her, and their eyes met. She stopped midsentence, searching for words.

"I've already had…m-my breakfast." She stared into his eyes, and he couldn't quite break the connection. She was so pretty in the morning, her face a ray of sunshine, her blond hair curling down her shoulders. She wore a red-plaid shirt and jeans and looked like she fit in around here. Too much.

"Excuse me," she said. "I'll come back a…a little later. It's nothing important." She turned, and before Lily or his mom could stop her, she was out the door.

"Crap." Cade pushed away from the table and went after her. He hated seeing the indecision on her face. He didn't want her to feel unwelcome in their home. His mom and Lily adored her, and that should be enough. But obviously it wasn't.

"Harper, wait," he called out.

She kept walking, out the front door and down the path. When she finally got far enough away from the house, her shoulders slumped and she turned around. "Why are you following me?"

"Why did you run off just then? We were all having coffee. You could've joined us."

"I don't want to break the terms of our agreement." Her chin went up.

"I think you're taking that a little bit too literally. We're bound to see each other around the house, the grounds. In the morning at breakfast, in the evening at dinner."

"You mean you'll actually have dinner with me, and not make other dates."

"I had that date on the books before you got here."

"Who was she?"

"*She* is a friend and her father is a business associate. She's nothing like you."

Harper squeezed her eyes closed and turned to walk away.

He stood his ground. "I meant that as a compliment to you."

She turned. "Your compliments are sorely lacking, Cade."

He grinned. He hadn't done that in a long while. "You're just as sassy as ever."

She lifted a shoulder and smiled back. "Can't help it."

"I know." He'd always liked that about her. "Want to go for a ride later? After work and before dinner?"

"Ride?"

"On Sage?"

Her face lit up at the mention of his mare. "I'm going to be busy all day."

"Can't you plan to be unbusy for an hour?"

"I, uh…"

"Come on. I want you to feel comfortable around here. There's no reason you have to leave a room every time I come into it."

"So, how does riding help?"

"You'll just have to wait and see."

"I have a lot of ordering for the party to do today. And I might have to go into town to do some shopping of my own."

"I'll tell you what. I'm going to be at the stables at five o'clock. If you can make it, fine. If not, just text me."

"Okay. That sounds fair."

"I'm going up to get ready for work," he said. "It's safe for you to go have breakfast with Mom and Lily now."

She rolled her eyes. "Cade, sometimes you make me crazy."

"Yeah, well. Welcome to my world."

Harper sat in the car, Lily in the driver seat, as they headed home from their trip into town. "I feel like we really accomplished a lot this afternoon," her friend said.

"We did. Thanks for your help. I feel we're making good headway. And the chairs and table settings you picked out are beautiful. I can picture how it will all look in the backyard, Lil. It's going to be a grand party."

"I hope so. Gage is in charge of the music. His band promised to play some sentimental tunes as well as their usual country rock. I can't wait for you to meet him in person."

"Just think, I get to meet a superstar."

"To me, he's just one of my brothers."

"Last time I checked, most brothers don't have a bunch of Grammys and pack stadiums with swooning fans from all around the world."

"Would you believe when Gage started out, all he really wanted was to play music in local clubs. He loves what he does, and he once said, as long as the good Lord lets him continue to make music, that's all he would ask for."

"I get that. I'm pretty much the same. I just want to earn a decent living doing what I love to do. He sounds like a pretty levelheaded guy."

"Gage?" She laughed. "Hardly. He's cocky as all get-out, and won't hold back at busting anyone's chops. But fame didn't do that to him—he was born that way."

"Still, I can't wait to meet him."

Lily pulled up in front of the guesthouse, and Harper grabbed the bag of spices she'd picked up at a specialty store. Some were exotic flavors, others were staples, but all were necessary for the dishes she was going to prepare. "Thanks for the ride. And the company."

"Yeah, we done good. Only five days to go before the big party."

"I'll be ready."

"So, what are you going to do the rest of the afternoon?"

It was three o'clock. "Me, uh, maybe I'll go over my recipes. Maybe take a rest."

"I have a better idea. Why don't you go on that ride with Cade?"

"You know about that?" she squeaked.

"Not because you told me. I overhead Cade telling Nathan to have the horses ready later."

"I haven't agreed to go. I probably shouldn't. I won't."

"Who are you trying to convince of that, me or you?"

"You. Me." Her shoulders slumped. "I can't put myself through that, Lil."

"You claim you love my brother. Is that still true?"

She nibbled on her lip. She hated admitting it, even to her dear friend, because saying it aloud only made the hurt go deeper.

"Harper?"

"What?"

"Do you love Cade?"

She thought about how he'd been at the cabin, the sweet guy who couldn't cook a thing when she first met him. The guy who chopped wood bare-chested like nobody's business, who also fought and won his battle with grief there, too. The guy who'd shown her what real love was truly like. "Yes, oh God. Yes. I can't deny it."

"So why not fight for him? Why not forget about staying away from him? Give yourself a chance with him. If he didn't want it, he wouldn't have asked you to go riding with him."

"I think I bruise his ego when I run off whenever he shows up. He doesn't want me to feel unwelcome here at your home. That's all it is."

"That's a load of horse poop, Harp. Cade still cares about you. He may not be over what happened yet, but won't you be sorry if you leave here never knowing? If you let him go without a fight?"

"Lily, why do you have to make so much sense all the time?"

"Go, Harper. If nothing else, enjoy a peaceful ride with a handsome hunk."

"*Hunk?* He's your brother."

"Ew, that did sound weird, but you know what I mean."

"I do. Cade *is* a hunk. I'll give it some thought, Lil. See you at dinner."

As soon as Cade sauntered over to her by the corral, Harper's mouth opened, and she hoped to high heaven there was no drool dripping out the sides. He was holding the reins of Sage and Cinnamon, wearing boots, jeans, a black snap-down shirt and a Stetson. He was her cowboy fantasy come to life, and it wasn't fair that Cade could have such an effect on her.

She wasn't made of stone. How could the man completely unravel her with just one look?

"Hello," she said, a bit tongue-tied.

"Hi. I'm glad you came."

She nodded. "I had a productive day. So, I'm here, but I have to warn you, I haven't ridden a horse since I was ten years old. And then it was one of those rides where you go round and round in a big circle."

"Sage is a real sweetheart. She won't give you any trouble. And I'll be right beside you."

She snapped her eyes to his, and his mouth twitched in that beautiful way she remembered. A stream of warmth coursed through her belly, making her giddy. "G-good to know."

"When you're ready, put your left boot into the stirrup, grab the saddle horn and then swing your leg around."

She attempted that easy feat three times before turning to Cade. "Epic fail."

"Nope. You just need a little boost. Try it again."

This time, when she tried to grab the saddle horn, Cade was behind her, giving her butt a steady boost up, so that she could swing her leg around and mount the horse.

"There you go," he said.

"Thanks." Her rear end tingled from his touch, and her mind went to places it shouldn't go.

He adjusted her stirrups and handed her the reins. He mounted Cinnamon, all the while giving Harper instructions on how to hold the reins and make the horse turn left or right or halt. "Got it," she said, though she didn't feel as confident as she sounded.

Cade made a clicking sound, and both horses took off at a slow gait.

The sun was warm on her shoulders, the sky a splash of colorful blues. "There's nothing like seeing the ranch on horseback," Cade said, seeming to think aloud.

Sage kept up with Cinnamon, so they rode side by side. "It's pretty this time of day."

Cade nodded. "It is."

She'd promised herself she wouldn't ask Cade why he'd asked her on this ride, so she held her tongue and let him steer the conversation. Only, he didn't say much. Instead, he simply rode quietly until they were in a silent rhythm with each other. The house was no longer in view, and they came upon a little stream running over a rocky creek bed. Trees shaded the entire area. It was a lovely spot.

"We'll stop here and water the horses."

He dismounted, then came over to her, his arms up, waiting to catch her if she fell. She managed to climb down off the horse without incident, and Cade put his arms down. "Good job," he said. They walked to the creek bed, and the horses followed, finding their way to water.

"This is my favorite spot on the entire ranch."

"I can see why. It's lovely here."

"You really think so?"

"I do," she said quietly.

"I once thought I'd build a house here. Something

smaller than the main house. Just big enough for a family."

"You were gonna build a house here for you and Bree." She sighed and turned away from him, so he wouldn't see what was in her eyes. He wouldn't see the hurt in her expression. They say, fake it until you make it. But she couldn't fake her feelings anymore. She couldn't pretend it didn't hurt being out here with Cade. She couldn't compete with angelic Bree.

He grabbed her hand, and she whipped her head around to meet his eyes. They were dark, brooding, filled with regret. "No. Actually, I wasn't. The idea came to me later, while at the cabin."

"While at the cabin?" Her voice squeaked. "You mean when you were a boy?"

"Not when I was a boy, Harper."

"Oh."

"I shouldn't have told you that," he rushed out, looking away. Looking like he wished he'd never spoken those words.

"There was no reason to," she whispered back. It only proved what she already knew: she'd blown it with him.

"No," he said, pulling her closer, giving the hand he held a gentle squeeze. "No reason at all," he said quietly.

Their chests collided, and Cade focused on her lips. He ran his other hand along her jawline, and the simple caress turned her insides upside down.

"Cade?"

"Shh."

Then he brought his mouth down on hers, and the touch of his lips to hers was like a bright spark on a dark, gloomy night. It connected them, made them whole again. It was scary good, delicious and amazing all at once.

Cade cupped her face in both hands and positioned her mouth to his. He devoured her, parting her lips, his tongue sweeping through her mouth until all she could do was whimper and moan.

Cade kissed her while walking her backward until she came up against a tree. He pressed his hard body to hers, and the friction was heaven on earth. He caressed her breasts through the material of her blouse until she wanted to scream. Then he moved his hand lower, teasing her below the waist, and she arched into his touch, trying to absorb the full impact of the pleasure he created through the soft denim. She heard her jeans zipper slowly being unfastened, the teeth spreading open, inviting Cade in. His hand flat against her, he pushed aside her panties and caressed her folds, the skin sensitive, pulsing. She was on the brink, unable to hold back. "Cade."

She gritted her teeth, and her body splintered in a release that shook her to the core. It was earth-shattering, and a few moments ticked by as she came down from this high.

Cade seemed pleased. He kissed her again and again and whispered, "Dawn."

Dawn? In the heat of passion, he called her Dawn. She backed away to gauge his eyes, but he was distracted by his phone. It rang and rang.

He stared at her for a long moment, blinking.

"You better get that," she said, suddenly confused and sinking fast.

He finally answered the call. "Lily, what the hell?"

She overheard Lily's panicked voice. "It's Mom, Cade. She took a fall down the stairs."

"Damn it. How is she?"

"She's pretty banged up and refusing to go to the hospital. She won't let me call an ambulance."

"Okay, I'll be right there." He hung up the phone and shook his head. "We've gotta go. My mama's hurt," he said, walking away to retrieve the horses.

"Oh no," she gasped. She ran over to Sage and tried to mount her, but Cade was there, hoisting her up none too gently.

Cade grabbed both of their reins. "Hold on to the saddle horn tight."

Then they took off at quick gait. Cade kept checking to make sure she was holding on, not losing her balance. He probably didn't want to have another fall on his hands. When the Tremaine home came into view from a distance, she called to him. "Cade, I'm slowing you down. I can get back from here. Hand me the reins."

"You sure?"

She nodded. "I'll walk Sage back. You go."

"Okay. Thanks."

She took hold of the reins and watched as Cade put his head down low to the mare's mane and flew like the wind. There was nothing that man couldn't do perfectly—except maybe get her name right.

That bothered her more than it should. It was as if he wanted Dawn, not Harper, and couldn't seem to see them both as the same person.

Her feelings were all jumbled up. She didn't know where she stood with Cade, but that didn't matter now. All that mattered was that Rose Tremaine would be okay.

Nine

Cade had taken his life in his hands when he threatened to cancel his mother's big birthday bash if she wouldn't let their family doctor take a look at her. Nobody threatened his mother and lived to tell about it. She was a force to be reckoned with. As it was, three days later, his mom was still barely talking to him. Luckily, she'd only fallen down three steps, not the entire flight of stairs. She'd bruised her legs pretty badly, and her knee had swelled up. Her cheek had been scraped where she'd hit the banister, and an eggplant-colored bruise popped up there. Nothing a bit of makeup wouldn't cover, or so she claimed. Nothing was going to stop her birthday party from happening. She was looking forward to having her entire family home. And that was that.

Lily, the sneak, had laid their mother's recovery all on Cade, claiming she had too much to do for the party. According to Dr. Adams, a few days of rest was all Rose needed and then she could dance at her own party. The doctor was an invited guest, so he'd be in attendance if anything else happened.

Irene made his mother's meals, and Cade brought them up to her in the morning before work and in the evening after he got home. It wasn't an ideal situation, but Rose wouldn't trust anyone but Cade with her recovery. He got her out of bed every morning and helped her walk around her room. Her knee still bothered her, but the meds the doctor had given her helped with the swelling.

Cade glanced out the window of his mother's room. The stables were in view, and he spotted a pretty blonde walking alongside the road...with Gage? When did his brother arrive home? Cade hadn't seen him yet, but he was sure talking up a storm with Harper. The two had their heads together, looking too close for comfort. Damn. Cade hadn't spoken to Harper since the night of the accident. He'd only texted her about his mother's condition. She'd said all the right things in her reply about how glad she was it wasn't more serious, and how she hoped Rose would be better in time for her party. But that's where it had ended.

"Mom, when did Gage get here?"

His mother looked surprised. "I didn't know he was."

"Well, he is. He'll probably be up soon to see you."

That's if he'd tear himself away from Harper long enough to visit his mother before she went to bed.

"Good. At least he won't fault me for wanting to have fun at my party."

"Mom, are you still mad at me?"

He continued to gaze out the window. Gage had enough charm to sweep any woman off her feet, and Harper seemed to be enjoying his attention. What girl wouldn't want to meet Gage Tremaine, superstar?

"I wasn't really mad, Cade. I was angry at myself for being clumsy and for everyone insisting I go to the hospital when I knew I didn't need to. But just so you know, if you ever speak to me that way again, I'll disown you," she added for good measure.

"That's nice, Mom," he replied, distracted. Gage and Harper had stopped by the corral fence from what he could see, having a fun ole time. What in hell did they have to talk about?

"Nice?" his mother asked. "Cade, you're not listening to a word I'm saying. Who's out there with Gage? Must be Harper. She's the only one who seems to hold your attention lately."

"Wh-what, Mom?"

"Cade, look at me."

He turned, shaking his head. "What is it, Mom?"

His mother smiled as if she knew a secret no one else did. And she was going to share it with him. "If your brain and your heart are in a battle, always go with your heart."

"It's not that simple. I still have issues with her."

"You're thinking too much. Harper is a talented,

sweet and smart girl. If you care for her, let her know. And if you don't, let her go."

Cade took one last glance out the window. It looked as if Gage and Harper were finally saying their goodbyes. Gage headed toward the main house and Harper toward the guesthouse. The relief Cade felt seeing them go their separate ways rattled him.

"Mom, I don't want to make another mistake."

"I get that you were injured when Bree died."

"This isn't about Bree anymore, Mom. It's about trust. I'm struggling with trusting again, and I don't know if I can trust Harper."

"Have you noticed the way she looks at you? Now, that's a woman who knows what she wants."

Cade sighed. If only he could have faith in that, in her.

"Son, I'm getting a little tired. Will you round up your brother and bring him in to see me before I turn in?"

"Sure, Mom."

"And, Cade. Think about what I said."

"Will do."

Harper was all he had been thinking about lately. He didn't need his mother to tell him that. He felt guilty leaving Harper in the lurch when his mother had been injured and not calling her afterward. The truth was, he'd been shaken to the core by their encounter at the creek, unable to halt his desire for her. Was it only about sex? Was he missing her, Harper, or was he simply fantasizing about Dawn, the girl he'd met and fallen for at the cabin?

Cade opened the front door just as Gage was walking in. "Hey, dude, good to see you." Gage smiled and opened his arms and the two bear-hugged. "It's been, what? Three months?"

"Something like that." They resembled each other, with their strong jawlines and thick shocks of dark hair. Both were over six feet tall, too. But Gage had blue eyes that all his fans seemed to think were dreamy. "It's good to see you, too. Mom's upstairs, getting ready to turn in."

"How is she?"

"Doing well. It's been murder getting her to take it easy, but I think she's gonna dance at her own party tomorrow night."

"Ah, I'm so glad. Would've been here sooner, but I had to do an interview in Houston. Man, I'm glad my tour's almost done."

"Well, it's good to have you home."

"Thanks, bro. Hey, I met your girl outside. Harper? She's real nice."

Cade folded his arms across his chest. "She's not my girl, Gage."

"She's not? Man, maybe she should be. She's got a lot going for her."

"What does that mean?"

"Hey, I follow the headlines. Hell, half the time, I'm the one in them. But Harper, she got a raw deal."

"She told you that? But you just met her."

"Don't get your panties in a knot," Gage said, grinning. "I watched the show. Whenever I could. And Harper and that Chef Dale guy weren't right for each other. The fans turned on her just because she recognized that fact before she made a big mistake in marrying him."

Cade's mouth tightened. Now he was getting romance advice from Gage, the guy who'd broken more than a few hearts in his day.

"If you're not interested in her, then maybe I—"

"Forget it, Gage." His brother was trying to bust his chops. That's all it was. They'd grown up competing with each other, but never over a woman. "Just so we're clear—Harper is off-limits."

"Yeah, I figured," he said, his mouth twitching in the start of a smile.

"You haven't changed."

"Why should I? I like who I am. Do you?"

No, Cade didn't like who he was right now. He liked the man he was at the cabin, a trusting soul who'd fallen in love with a wonderful woman. "Mom's waiting for you. Let's have a drink together later?"

"Sure, I'm always up for that."

Harper couldn't believe she'd just met Gage Tremaine. He was larger than life, and when he'd introduced himself to her over by the stables, she had to admit she'd had a fangirl moment. But it had only taken a few minutes talking to him to learn two things about Gage. First, underneath the heartbreaker superstar facade was a decent man who cared a good deal about his family. Second, Gage wasn't Cade. Not by a long shot. And thinking of Gage's brother only made her hurt even more. Because in two days, she'd be leaving, and her time with Cade Tremaine would be over.

She made herself a cup of tea and plunked down on the sofa, staring at the television, not really paying attention to what was happening on the screen. Tomorrow was the big day, and she needed to get a good night's sleep. She'd exhausted herself, but in a good way, training her sous chefs and going through a dry run with the staff to make sure everything would work like clockwork for the party. She put all else out of her mind, focusing solely on her job. The menu was set and all deliveries had been made. Now, it was just a matter of creating a delectable meal with all the trimmings.

The knock on her door startled her. She wasn't up to visitors. She was exhausted and totally unpresentable, wearing gray sweatpants with her greasy hair piled atop her head. She thought about not answering the door, but the knocking was persistent and she had a pretty good idea who it was.

"Just a minute," she called out. She ran into the bathroom, washed her face and brushed her teeth, then groaned at her reflection in the mirror.

"Harper, are you okay in there?" Cade called out.

"Fine," she said, and walked over to the door. Cade was the very last person on earth she wanted to see right now. She whipped open the door. "What?"

He looked her over from top to bottom, and his expression didn't change. "Hi."

"Hello," she said, folding her arms.

"Sorry to bother you so late."

"It is late."

"Will you invite me in?"

She shook her head. "No."

"I get why you're mad, Harper. I shouldn't have…"

"Why are you here, Cade? For a man who sets down rules, you certainly don't abide by them."

"I know. I've been—"

"Confused? Hurt? Unsure? Well, so am I. But I'm one other thing. I'm exhausted and not up for this, Cade. I have a big day tomorrow. So, I'm going to say good night now."

"Harper?"

"Glad you got my name right this time." She closed the door, pretty much in his face.

Which only made her feel worse, instead of better.

Ten

Saturday morning, Harper, dressed in chef's whites, was sitting in the dining room with Rose, Lily and Gage. "I'm glad you joined us for breakfast," Rose said. "You've been working very hard this week."

"Thank you. It's great to see you up and around."

"I'm up and ready for my party," she said, taking a sip of coffee. "I'm only sad my dear friend Tonette won't be coming. She's very ill and her daughter, Gianna, is taking care of her. I'm afraid my friend isn't…" Tears came to Rose's eyes. She couldn't say any more.

"Oh, Rose, I'm so sorry to hear that," Harper said.

Rose was such a strong woman, but Lily had said Tonette's illness had taken a toll on her. The two were like sisters.

"Mom, Gianna is with her. Tonette understands. We'll visit her next week," Lily said. "Just like we always do. I promise."

"Okay. Thanks, honey. I enjoy our visits." She patted Lily's hand. "Do you know where Cade is? I thought he would've come down by now."

Irene served them bacon and eggs, and, according to the Tremaine cook, Gage's favorite: yeast rolls. Apparently, she wasn't wrong. Gage grabbed three rolls and buttered them like a pro.

"I wouldn't be expecting him for breakfast," Gage said. "He sorta drank me under the table last night."

"Geesh," Lily said. "You guys with your drinking games."

"Not games, sis. We're not eighteen anymore. He did some serious damage, then went up to bed."

All eyes turned to Harper, and she put her head down, trying to keep heat from burning her cheeks. She hadn't been hungry before she sat down, being too excited to start the day with her sous chefs and prepping the meal. But now, her stomach churned and she surely couldn't bear to take a bite of anything. She slugged her coffee down in a big gulp.

"Harper, why don't you tell Gage about the menu you planned for tonight."

"Oh, sure," she said, grateful for the change of subject. "Keeping with the surf and turf theme, we'll start out with bourbon-and-pineapple steak-and-shrimp kabobs, among half a dozen other appetizers."

"You could stop right there," Gage said, "and I'd be happy."

"Oh, hush," Rose told Gage. "Let the girl finish."

Gage winked at her. "Sorry, Harper. Please go on."

She gave him a smile. "We'll be baking fresh, rustic sourdough bread for the table. And then serving a cranberry-pecan salad with raspberry vinaigrette. And the main dish is prime rib roast, served with a side of linguine with scallops and artichoke hearts in a white wine cream sauce."

"My stomach's grumbling already. I'm impressed," Gage said.

"Me too," Lily said. "Harper's a great chef. Her food always tastes so delicious. She even taught Cade to cook, if you can believe that."

"Cade cooking? Now, I'm really impressed. Maybe you can teach me, too, Harper. I can hardly toast bread."

Harper looked at Lily and she shrugged. "What can I say? My brothers are hopeless in the kitchen."

"Or maybe just hopeless," Cade interjected, and all eyes turned to the doorway.

"Well, speak of the devil," Gage said.

Cade sauntered into the room, looking like he'd had a rough night. His hair was rumpled, his eyes bloodshot, and his clothes a wrinkled mess. Always at first sight of him, love surged inside Harper, softening her heart. And then she remembered all that had transpired between them. Last night, she'd spoken harshly to him and sent him packing. She had every right to do that. He couldn't come in and out of her life as he pleased. She was glad she'd spoken her mind, yet she did feel a bit guilty, looking at the wreck he was this morning.

"Cade, come sit and have some coffee with us," Rose said. "Looks like you need it."

Cade gave everyone a glance, then stopped on Harper, noting her chef's uniform. "Morning," he said to her.

"Good morning," she replied.

"Big day?"

She nodded. "For everyone. Actually, I should get started in the kitchen. The crew will be here in half an hour." She rose from the table. "Thanks for breakfast."

Cade's mouth twisted in a frown. This time she wasn't trying to avoid him. "I really have to start work," she told everyone, making her point to Cade, as well.

"Of course you do," Rose said. "But be sure to take a break every once in a while. You didn't eat a thing for breakfast."

"I'll eat later, I promise."

"I'll join you in the kitchen in a few minutes," Lily said.

"I'm counting on it," she told Lily.

She was just outside the door when she overheard Cade say to his brother, "And no, she's not gonna teach you how to cook."

Harper rolled her eyes, but then the more she thought about it, the more it made her smile.

Harper spent the morning working hard with her staff to prep the meal. She chopped vegetables, sampled the meat and scallops for taste and texture, and made sauces and marinades. She worked on a fruit tower, using some secrets she'd learned in culinary school to make it stand over two feet tall.

Outside, in the backyard, tables were being set up. She heard Gage and his band members constructing a stage and doing sound checks.

A flower delivery arrived, including bouquets of pastel roses to decorate the first floor of the house, while a dozen arrangements for the tables were placed in the dining room to keep cool until just before the party started at six o'clock.

Lily was in and out of the kitchen all day, helping as much as she could until she was called away to check on something else. By one in the afternoon, Harper felt like it was all coming together. She watched her team work and was proud of the job they were doing.

To her surprise, Cade walked into the kitchen, dressed in sharp clothes, his eyes keenly alert. The transformation from morning to afternoon was truly stunning. Again, her traitorous heart did an Olympic-quality somersault.

"I've never seen you in your chef's whites," Cade said. "I like it."

"Thanks." She continued chopping bell peppers.

"How's it going?" he asked, glancing at the half dozen sous chefs working in the kitchen.

"Well, we're right on target, so you can report back to Lily all is going smoothly."

"That's not why I'm here."

She kept her head down, finding more veggies to chop. "Oh no?"

"I came to ask you to give me some time after the party. I'd like to speak with you privately."

"Cade."

"I mean it, Harper. We really need to talk. Just give me twenty minutes of your time."

"I don't know." She gestured to the room with all its organized chaos. "I can't think clearly right now."

"That's why I want to see you after this is all over."

"Okay. Fine. I'll see you after the party."

A smile crossed his face, one that melted her silly, stupid heart. "Great. I'll see you soon."

By late afternoon, the kitchen was abuzz. Guests would begin arriving in minutes, and Harper and her team were ready. She couldn't be prouder of the way they'd worked together these past few days. With the clinking of a glass, she summoned their attention, and they gathered around. "I just want to thank you all for your hard work this week. I couldn't have asked for a better team to work with. We've accomplished quite a bit, and everything is looking great. So again, thank you from the bottom of my heart. It's the witching hour now, the party's about to begin and we've got more to do. So, let's all get busy."

Lily walked in with Rose, both looking glamorous in long shimmering gowns. Rose was walking without a limp, a regal picture in soft pink. She beamed from ear to ear. "This all looks marvelous," she said, glancing at the food.

"Thanks, but you're the one who looks marvelous. Both of you do."

"Mom's about ready to greet her guests. But she insisted on seeing you first."

"Harper," Rose said. "I'm so happy you're here. You've taken over the kitchen and done a professional job. I can tell already it's going to be truly wonderful. I only wish you could attend the party instead of working in here all night."

"Rose, that means the world to me. Thank you."

"Mom, I'll make sure Harper gets some time at the party."

"You do that, Lily."

After they walked out, Harper looked down at her chef's uniform and grimaced. She was a total mess, with grease stains and raspberry smudges covering her entire coat. She excused herself and walked out the door, heading for the guesthouse, where a fresh white coat was ready to go.

A valet was opening car doors in front of the house, and she came face-to-face with a red-haired woman just exiting her car. She was striking, supermodel-sleek, wearing an emerald green gown with a plunging neckline.

"Oh, hello," the woman said to her. "You're Harper Dawn, aren't you?"

"Uh, yes, I am." Harper had trouble not staring at the woman's impeccable features.

"Cade did say you were catering the party tonight. I'm Madeline O'Shea." She put out her hand. "A very good friend of Cade's—and the family, of course."

Madeline? She remembered Lily telling her something about Cade's ex-girlfriend. She was pre-Bree and, if she recalled correctly, someone Lily wasn't too fond of.

Harper slid her hands down her coat to wipe them clean before taking the woman's hand. "Nice to meet you."

"I recognized you from the reality show," she said. "I'm a loyal fan of *One Last Date*. But Cade never would watch it. He thought it was insane and thought any woman who had to go on a reality show to find love was well...*I'm too nice to say.* He hated being dragged into that whole mess with you. He as much as told me so over dinner the other night."

Harper hadn't spent weeks on *One Last Date* not to recognize a woman with her claws out. Madeline was staking a claim on Cade. But it was news to her that Cade had taken Madeline out to dinner while she was waiting for a call from him. Oh boy, she was such a fool. She'd always vowed not to let women like Madeline get the best of her, but wow, she was good. And from the wicked smile on her face, Madeline knew it.

"If you'll excuse me, I have to go." Harper brushed past her, holding in her anger, her rage, but she couldn't quite shelve her pain. It spread through her body like wildfire.

Once she arrived back to the kitchen in a pristine white coat and wearing a toque on her head, she had calmed down somewhat. The party had started, and she focused on overseeing the serving of the appetizers.

Lily wandered into the kitchen twenty minutes later. "Hi, just checking in. Everything's going smoothly out there. I'm hearing good things from the guests."

Harper gave her a solemn nod as she sliced freshly baked bread with a vengeance. "Thanks."

"Harper, what's wrong? I can tell you're not happy. What's going on?"

"It's nothing."

"It is something. I know that look. Remember, you can't fool me. I'm your bestie since college, and we know each other inside out."

She shrugged and set down her knife. "Nothing I want to talk about."

Lily grabbed her arm and tugged her out of the kitchen and into the downstairs study, where Lily gave her a stern speak-to-me look. "Something's wrong. What is it?"

She sighed. "What do you know about Madeline O'Shea?"

Lily blinked a few times. "You want to know about Madeline?"

"Yes, I met her a bit ago and…"

"She gave you grief," Lily finished for her. "The truth is, Madeline's never gotten over losing my brother to Bree. She's been after Cade ever since Bree passed away."

"You mean, Cade dumped her for Bree?"

"*Dumped* isn't the right word. They weren't getting along and Cade realized she wasn't the woman for him. She did not take the breakup well. Shortly after, Cade started seeing Bree."

"Madeline told me she went out to dinner with Cade this week. Did you know about that?"

"I wouldn't worry. Cade does business with her father, and so he sees her occasionally. But it always seems to be about business."

"But you're not sure?"

"I'm sure of Cade. He's crazy about you, Harper. I wouldn't give up on him."

"Does he know he's crazy about me?"

Lily grinned. "Probably not, but Gage and Mom seem to think so, too."

Harper rolled her eyes. What good was it that they all thought so, if Cade was too blind or gun shy to know it? "Lil, I've gotta get back to work. Thanks for the talk."

"Sure, any time." Lily kissed her cheek. "You're kicking butt out there, girl. I'm so proud of you."

Harper returned to the kitchen, feeling slightly better. Her sous chefs were all giddy listening to Gage Tremaine sing as they prepared the meals. He had a dynamic voice that streamed into the house. His tone was unique, and it was no wonder he'd become such a superstar. But he'd had his share of scandals lately. Though the Gage she'd met hardly seemed to be such a bad boy. And Lily claimed he was innocent of most things written about him in the tabloids.

Harper could relate.

She kept busy throughout the evening, making

sure the dishes were going out on time, hearing the rumble of conversations mingling with music and laughter. It put her in a good mood. She liked Rose, who was definitely a powerful woman with a soft spot for her children. She deserved to celebrate her birthday in the best of ways, surrounded by family and good friends. All 150 of them.

After all the meals were served and dinner was over, Harper breathed a sigh of relief. All they had to do now was sing "Happy Birthday" to Rose and have cake and the other desserts the pastry chef had cooked up, and her work would be done.

It was a bittersweet moment, having accomplished so much while she also felt so unsettled. She walked over to the double French doors, opening one to hear the full power of Gage's sultry, deep voice. When the song ended, Gage looked out onto the crowd, finding his mother sitting at a table with her friends. He spoke into the microphone, "Mom, it's your turn on stage now. Come on up. Cade, Lily and I have something special for you."

Harper had to see this. She'd promised Lily she'd come outside the second her work was done. She unbuttoned her white coat and took off her hat, fussing with her hair a bit and straightening out the dress that had been crushed under her uniform. Then she walked out onto the patio. The stage was set back and illuminated with several strategically placed spotlights. Overhead, twinkle lights sparkled.

Lily took her mom's arm, while Cade took the other and they escorted her up on stage. The cake was brought over on a cart and placed in front of the stage so everyone could view it. It was a true work of art, thanks to the pastry chef Harper had hired.

"So, what do you get a mom who has everything?" Gage asked the crowd while taking his mother's hand. Rose gazed into Gage's eyes in a tender moment. "You have all three of your kids sing you a birthday song. One that was written just for you."

The crowd let out a collective sigh. Tears formed in Harper's eyes at the love all three had for their mother.

Gage played the guitar and did most of the singing with Cade and Lily as backup. The ballad was touching and emotional, creating an unforgettable moment. And when it was over, they were all given a standing ovation. "Happy birthday, Mom," they said over the applause, each one giving Rose a kiss on the cheek.

Harper clapped so hard her hands hurt and then made her way over to Rose and Lily by the stage. "Happy birthday, Rose." She kissed her cheek, too.

"Oh, Harper, thank you. The meal was delicious. I can't tell you how many people complimented the food. Everything was superb."

"I'm happy to hear that."

The band played on, and Gage approached the three of them. "Mom, can I have this dance?"

"Of course, son. Excuse me," Rose said, smiling. "My son wants to dance with me."

"You go, Mom."

"Have fun," Harper said.

A few seconds later, Nathan came over to say

hello, his focus on Lily. He seemed to hang on her every word, and then he quite tactfully asked, "Would one of you ladies care to dance?"

Harper took a step back. "You go on, Lil. I'm so tired I can barely stand, much less dance."

"You're sure?"

"Of course. Go on, Nathan, take Lily around the dance floor."

Harper found a wall to lean against to watch the festivities. Even though she was tired of being on her feet, she tapped her foot in tune with the country sounds, finally able to enjoy the party. Several of the Tremaines' friends made a special effort to come over to compliment her meal, explaining Rose had pointed her out to them. And not a one of them mentioned seeing her on *One Last Date*, thank goodness. It was a triumphant moment, boosting her spirits and inspiring her to finish her cookbook.

She looked around, searching for Cade. He seemed to have disappeared after the birthday song. Unfortunately, her search ended when he suddenly appeared on the dance floor with Madeline's arms draped around his neck, her body crushed to his. Even though the music was upbeat, they moved slowly, as if they'd shut out the entire world. And then Cade kissed her, right there on the dance floor, in front of everyone. Harper didn't know how long the kiss lasted; she wasn't about to wait around to find out.

All she knew was that her heart had finally shattered, and there was no hope left. This whole mess was finally over. She walked into the kitchen to give it one final inspection. Luckily her staff had taken care of everything. She didn't have one more obligation to the Tremaine family, so she grabbed her things and walked straight out the front door.

Cade searched the crowd for Harper. He wanted to spend at least a few minutes with her during the party, but he couldn't find her. He approached Gage and his mom. "Have you seen Harper anywhere? She's not in the kitchen and her staff hasn't seen her, either."

"Nope. I haven't seen her," Gage said, shaking his head. "But you better hope she didn't see you with Madeline. That was not cool, bro. What in hell is going on with you?"

"*Madeline?* You think she saw me with Madeline?"

"Everyone near the dance floor saw you locking lips with her," his mother said, condemnation in her voice.

"It's not what you think. Hell, that woman causes nothing but trouble. She's a damn drama queen."

"I hope you're not talking about Harper," his mother said.

Lily approached, her expression grim and aimed directly at him. "What did you do now?"

"Why, where's Harper?"

"She's at the guesthouse. She wants to leave, ASAP. But she doesn't have a car and she won't ask me to leave Mom's party early. I'm supposed to take her home first thing in the morning, A-hole." Lily looked toward her mother. "Sorry, Mom."

"It's okay, honey. I agree."

All eyes turned to Cade.

"Are you going to let that girl go?" his mother asked.

"Man, she's a keeper, Cade," Gage said, shaking his head, giving him a don't-be-a-dumbass look. "Even I recognize that."

"I know. I know." Cade's gut clenched. He might have blown it with Harper for good, and that would be the worst thing that ever happened to him. Well, except for losing Bree. But losing Harper was right up there on the same level. "I need to talk to her."

"She doesn't want to talk to you. She texted me specifically to keep you away from her."

"I have to see her. Tonight. Give me your phone, Lily."

"No way."

"Cade, what are you up to?" his mother asked suspiciously.

"I just need to explain. And straighten all this out. But I can't do it without Lily's phone and her car keys."

"Now you want my keys?"

"If you want your best friend becoming a part of this family, you'll give them up."

"Really?" Lily grinned, and her entire demeanor changed.

"Man, you have it bad," Gage said. "Take pity on the guy and give him what he wants, sis. Or we'll never hear the end of it."

"Okay, but if you do anything to hurt her, I'll never forgive you," Lily warned.

"And I'll disown you," his mom said, halfway serious.

"Then I'll kick you to the curb like yesterday's garbage," Gage said, making his point.

"Got it. Now hand them over," Cade said, finally seeing some light.

He only hoped it wasn't too late.

Harper let the warm water of the shower rain down, cleaning her body of a full day in the kitchen. The grease, the oil, the scents of herbs and garlic all needed washing away. But so did her aching heart. She wished there was a shower for that. Something that could wipe away her uncontrollable sobs. Something that could free her body of fierce and unyielding pain. She could call Cade Tremaine a jerk, a fool, an idiot, but none of that seemed to make her feel any better. Because she still loved him. Desperately and helplessly. So didn't that make her the bigger fool? The grander idiot?

She let the warmth spread over her body until her tears no longer mingled with the water spraying down. Until the warmth gave her courage enough to face the cold reality that Cade was out of her life now.

For good.

She stepped out of the shower and dried off with a towel. Her phone buzzed on the countertop, and she picked it up to read a text from Lily. The party broke up early. I can take you home now, if you're set on leaving tonight.

It's late, Lil. I can't impose on you that way.

I'll spend the night at your place and drive home in the morning. No problem.

Harper glanced at the clock. It was ten thirty. She could be off Tremaine land and in her own bed before midnight. Nothing would make her happier. And Lily would be there in the morning to keep her company. Maybe to help nurse her wounds.

That's a good plan, she texted back. Thanks, my friend.

I'll be there in thirty minutes.

Harper made fast work of packing up her stuff. She didn't have all that much here, so it was easy to gather up her clothes and dump them into her suit-cases. Any regrets she had in leaving this place were stifled when the sight of Cade and Madeline kissing entered her mind. Something squeezed tight in her belly every time she thought about Cade. He'd prob-ably wanted to tell her he was getting back with Mad-eline when they were supposed to talk tonight. So, she was saving him the trouble.

Damn him.

The doorbell rang precisely thirty minutes later,

and she was more than ready. She grabbed her bags and glanced out the window to see Lily's car in the driveway. She opened the door. "I can't thank—" She gasped, stunned to find Cade at her threshold, not Lily. "What are you doing here?" She looked over his shoulder for Lily. "I'm waiting for your sister."

Cade took a deep breath, and his lips turned down. "Lily's not coming."

The look on his face frightened her. "Did something happen to her?"

"No, nothing like that. Lily is fine. Trust me."

She laughed in his face. What a joke, asking her to trust him. "I don't."

"I know. I'm sorry about that. That's why I'm here, to explain and make things right. I knew if I asked to speak with you, you'd slam the door in my face again."

"And you'd be right. I saw you tonight with Madeline. You kissed her on the dance floor. So, there's nothing more to explain. She made it clear how things are between you."

Cade's eyes darkened to coal, and his face twisted up at the mention of Madeline's name. "She had too much to drink. The next thing I know, she's dragging me on the dance floor and kissing me. I didn't want to make a scene in front of all the guests. But if you saw the whole thing, you would've seen me give her a stern talking-to afterward. I made it clear that I wasn't interested in her that way and handed her over to her father. Regardless of what happens between you and me, I still wouldn't go back to Madeline."

He seemed sincere, and she took a moment to digest what he claimed had happened with Madeline. She wasn't going to deny that his explanation made sense. And maybe she'd jumped to conclusions a teeny, tiny bit too soon. Still, she had doubts. "You lied to me. You pretended to be Lily in the texts."

"And you lied to me for days, pretending to be someone you weren't."

"That's not entirely true, Cade. I am the same person I always was. And I've apologized for that many times."

"And I've forgiven you." He put out his hand. "Will you take a drive with me?"

That caught her off guard. "Why?"

"So we can talk. Really talk. I have something I want to show you. I'll take your suitcases and drive you back to Barrel Falls myself if you still want that after you hear me out."

Harper gave his proposition a moment of thought. It seemed like a win-win. If she didn't like his explanation, she'd be assured of going home tonight. It was the best she was going to get.

"Fine."

He grabbed her suitcases as she closed up the guesthouse and followed him to Lily's SUV. He hoisted both bags into the back end, then opened the car door for her. He was still such a gentleman. She was beginning to appreciate all that Southern charm.

Once she was seated and buckled up, Cade climbed in and started the engine. To her surprise, he whipped the car around, leading away from the main road and heading deeper onto Tremaine land.

She sat quietly, not asking any questions as they passed the stables and then took off down a bumpy path. One she recognized, perhaps. But it was dark out, the stars above giving only slight illumination. "You know, my family threatened to toss me out on my ass if I didn't go after you."

"Smart family. I like them all."

"They like you. Better than they like me, I think."

"So, is that what you're doing? Going after me?"

He turned to her and nodded. "It took me a while to figure some things out. I admit, I'm slow on the draw at times. Especially after I met a gorgeous brunette who wrapped me around her little finger. It was new to me, being with someone else. Giving of myself. One day, you were this sweet tomboy hiker and herb-loving chef, and the next day I find out you're one of the biggest reality stars in the country. It threw me off and made me really think about what I was doing with my own life."

He stopped the car a short distance from his favorite place by the stream and got out. She didn't wait for him to open the door for her, but when she exited the car, he took her hand. He faced her as they both leaned one shoulder against the car.

"Harper, I condemned you for going on that show. I shouldn't have. It was wrong. I shouldn't have judged you."

He touched a wisp of her hair and then gazed deep into her eyes. She was mesmerized, caught up in him, in this beautiful place. A few stars shined above, but it was enough to see the sincerity on his face. Her heart was racing; it hadn't stopped since the moment he showed up at the guesthouse.

"Why should you be any different than anyone else?"

"I should be different because I care deeply about you. I watched all ten episodes of *One Last Date*."

She gasped, her hand going to her mouth. She knew from Lily that he'd watched some of it, but he'd seen every second, every moment of what she'd gone through. "You saw it all? I wish you hadn't."

"I'm glad I did. I saw how you struggled with finding the right man, how much you wanted to find love. You weren't in it for the fame, to make a name for yourself, like some of the others. I could tell you were authentic. You put yourself out there, and it wasn't easy. But I was proud of you for sticking up for yourself when you realized you didn't love Dale, that though you had a lot in common, and he was perfect on paper, you couldn't see spending the rest of your life with him."

"Thank you. That means a lot to me."

"Sweetheart, how could I blame you for trying to find love over the course of a ten-week television program when I fell in love with you in less than a week over bad rummy games, hot, sweaty hikes and cooking lessons? Harper Dawn, I'm crazy in love with you."

"Oh, Cade," she breathed out softly. "I love you, too. So much." Tears misted in her eyes. And she touched his face to make sure this was real. "But are you sure you didn't just fall in love with Dawn by the lake?"

He grinned. "I fell in love with Dawn and with Harper. Even if I hadn't seen you on *One Last Date*, the woman you are today, standing right here in front of me, is the woman I love with my whole heart. I discovered that love can happen in the craziest ways, under unique circumstances. And I wouldn't change a minute of my time getting to know you."

"Are you sure?"

"I'll prove how sure I am, but first…"

He took her face in his hands and crushed his mouth to hers, kissing her like there was no tomorrow, kissing her like he could devour her. She'd never felt so loved, so incredibly joyous.

Cade ended the kiss and smiled, a big, wide over-the-moon kind of boyish smile. "C'mon," he said, taking her hand. He led her down a slope and there, hidden under the arching branches of two trees overlooking the stream, was a table set for two with white linens, flowers and a bottle of champagne in a silver bucket. Cade lit half a dozen small candles, and the table flickered to life. "I wanted to have our own private celebration tonight."

"Is this why you insisted we have a talk tonight?"

"I couldn't interrupt your work, Harper. I knew how much it meant to you. But I'm selfish enough to want you all to myself. Here in my favorite spot."

He pulled out a chair for her, and she sat down. He sat across from her and took her hand in his. Before he could speak, she had to ask, "The last time we were here was when your mom got hurt. Why didn't you call me after that?"

"I should have. But it was here that I realized how much I loved you. To be honest, it scared me a little. It wasn't about Bree anymore. It was about opening myself up again to that strong of an emotion. And Mom was hurt and needed my help, and there was the party. But Harper, sweetheart, I never meant to hurt you. I'm no expert in love, but I know now, you're the only woman for me."

Harper's eyes went wide, and she held her breath as Cade got down on one knee. "Harper Dawn, I love you more than I can put into words. But know I'll do everything in my power to make you happy. Will you marry me?"

It was her deepest wish to marry a man who loved her unconditionally. And Cade had proved that he did. He loved her through lies and deception and was man enough to see the woman she really was. "Cade, I couldn't be happier than I am right now. Yes, I'll marry you. I'll be your wife."

He placed his class ring on her finger. "I'll get you the ring of your dreams," Cade said, "but for now please accept this ring as my pledge of love."

Cade took both of her hands, and they rose together. "I don't need a new ring," she said softly, "when I have the *man* of my dreams right here."

Cade kissed her softly this time, sweetly. There was no longer any rush. They were bonded together through true love.

"What do you say about us building a house together? Right here, and you can design your own kitchen and finish that cookbook you're working on."

"It'll be a place for us to raise a family, Cade."

"I like the sound of that."

He kissed her again and then opened the champagne bottle, the cork popping and bubbles spilling out. They toasted to their future, and to Cade being her very own *one last date*.

* * * *

Don't miss bad boy superstar
Gage Tremaine's story
by USA TODAY *bestselling author*
Charlene Sands,
available August 2021 from Harlequin Desire!

WE HOPE YOU ENJOYED
THIS BOOK FROM

⬦ HARLEQUIN
DESIRE

*Luxury, scandal, desire—welcome to
the lives of the American elite.*

Be transported to the worlds of oil barons, family dynasties,
moguls and celebrities. Get ready for juicy plot twists,
delicious sensuality and intriguing scandal.

6 NEW BOOKS AVAILABLE EVERY MONTH!

#2797 THE MARRIAGE HE DEMANDS
Westmoreland Legacy: The Outlaws by Brenda Jackson
Wealthy Alaskan Cash Outlaw has inherited a ranch and needs land owned by beautiful, determined Brianna Banks. She'll sign it over with one condition: Cash fathering the child she desperately wants. But he won't be an absentee father and makes his own demand...

#2798 BLUE COLLAR BILLIONAIRE
Texas Cattleman's Club: Heir Apparent • by Karen Booth
After heartbreak, socialite Lexi Alderidge must focus on her career, not another relationship. But she makes an exception for the rugged worker at her family's construction site, Jack Bowden. Sparks fly, but is he the man she's assumed he is?

#2799 CONSEQUENCES OF PASSION
Locketts of Tuxedo Park • by Yahrah St. John
Heir to a football dynasty, playboy Roman Lockett is used to getting what he wants, but one passionate night with Shantel Wilson changes everything. Overwhelmed by his feelings, he tries to forget her—until he learns she's pregnant. Now he vows to claim his child...

#2800 TWIN GAMES IN MUSIC CITY
Dynasties: Beaumont Bay • by Jules Bennett
When music producer Will Sutherland signs country's biggest star, Hannah Banks, their mutual attraction is way too hot...so she switches with her twin to avoid him. But Will isn't one to play games—or let a scheming business rival ruin everything...

#2801 SIX NIGHTS OF SEDUCTION
by Maureen Child
CEO Noah Graystone cares about business and nothing else. Tired of being taken for granted, assistant Tessa Parker puts in her notice—but not before one last business trip with no-strings seduction on the schedule. Can their six hot nights turn into forever?

#2802 SO RIGHT...WITH MR. WRONG
The Serenghetti Brothers • by Anna DePalo
Independent fashion designer Mia Serenghetti needs the help of Damian Musil—son of the family that has been feuding with hers for years. But when one hot kiss leads to a passion neither expected, what will become of these star-crossed lovers?

SPECIAL EXCERPT FROM

⊕HARLEQUIN

DESIRE

Wealthy Alaskan Cash Outlaw has inherited a ranch and needs land owned by beautiful, determined Brianna Banks. She'll sign it over under one condition: Cash fathering the child she desperately wants. But he won't be an absentee father and makes his own demand...

Read on for a sneak peek at
The Marriage He Demands
by New York Times *bestselling author Brenda Jackson.*

"Are you really going to sell the Blazing Frontier without even taking the time to look at it? It's a beautiful place."

"I'm sure it is, but I have no need of a ranch, dude or otherwise."

"I think you're making a mistake, Cash."

Cash lifted a brow. Normally, he didn't care what any person, man or woman, thought about any decision he made, but for some reason what she thought mattered.

It shouldn't.

What he should do was thank her for joining him for lunch, and tell her not to walk back to Cavanaugh's office with him, although he knew both their cars were parked there. In other words, he should put as much distance between them as possible.

I can't.

Maybe it was the way her luscious mouth tightened when she was not happy about something. He'd picked up on it twice now. Lord help him but he didn't want to see it a third time. He'd rather see her smile, lick an ice cream cone or... lick him.

He quickly forced the last image from his mind, but not before a hum of lust shot through his veins. There had to be a reason he was so attracted to her. Maybe he could blame it on the Biggins deal Garth had closed just months before he'd gotten engaged to Regan. That had taken working endless days and nights, and for the past year Cash's social life had been practically nonexistent.

On the other hand, even without the Biggins deal as an excuse, there was strong sexual chemistry radiating between them. He felt it but honestly wasn't sure that even at twenty-seven she recognized it for what it was.

That was intriguing, to the point that he was tempted to hang around Black Crow another day. Besides, he was a businessman, and no businessman would sell or buy anything without checking it out first. He was letting his personal emotions around Ellen cloud what was usually a very sound business mind.

"You are right, Brianna. I would be making a mistake if I didn't at least see the ranch before selling it. Is now a good time?"

The huge smile that spread across her face was priceless… and mesmerizing. When was the last time a woman, any woman, had this kind of effect on him? When he felt spellbound? He concluded that never had a woman captivated him like Brianna Banks was doing.

Don't miss what happens next in
The Marriage He Demands
by Brenda Jackson, the next book in her
Westmoreland Legacy: The Outlaws series!

Available April 2021 wherever
Harlequin Desire books and ebooks are sold.

Harlequin.com

Get 4 FREE REWARDS!

We'll send you 2 FREE Books plus 2 FREE Mystery Gifts.

Harlequin Desire books transport you to the world of the American elite with juicy plot twists, delicious sensuality and intriguing scandal.

FREE
Value Over
$20

YES! Please send me 2 FREE Harlequin Desire novels and my 2 FREE gifts (gifts are worth about $10 retail). After receiving them, if I don't wish to receive any more books, I can return the shipping statement marked "cancel." If I don't cancel, I will receive 6 brand-new novels every month and be billed just $4.55 per book in the U.S. or $5.24 per book in Canada. That's a savings of at least 13% off the cover price! It's quite a bargain! Shipping and handling is just 50¢ per book in the U.S. and $1.25 per book in Canada.* I understand that accepting the 2 free books and gifts places me under no obligation to buy anything. I can always return a shipment and cancel at any time. The free books and gifts are mine to keep no matter what I decide.

225/326 HDN GNND

Name (please print)

Address   Apt. #

City   State/Province   Zip/Postal Code

Email: Please check this box ☐ if you would like to receive newsletters and promotional emails from Harlequin Enterprises ULC and its affiliates. You can unsubscribe anytime.

Mail to the **Harlequin Reader Service:**
IN U.S.A.: P.O. Box 1341, Buffalo, NY 14240-8531
IN CANADA: P.O. Box 603, Fort Erie, Ontario L2A 5X3

Want to try 2 free books from another series? Call 1-800-873-8635 or visit www.ReaderService.com.

*Terms and prices subject to change without notice. Prices do not include sales taxes, which will be charged (if applicable) based on your state or country of residence. Canadian residents will be charged applicable taxes. Offer not valid in Quebec. This offer is limited to one order per household. Books received may not be as shown. Not valid for current subscribers to Harlequin Desire books. All orders subject to approval. Credit or debit balances in a customer's account(s) may be offset by any other outstanding balance owed by or to the customer. Please allow 4 to 6 weeks for delivery. Offer available while quantities last.

Your Privacy—Your information is being collected by Harlequin Enterprises ULC, operating as Harlequin Reader Service. For a complete summary of the information we collect, how we use this information and to whom it is disclosed, please visit our privacy notice located at corporate.harlequin.com/privacy-notice. From time to time we may also exchange your personal information with reputable third parties. If you wish to opt out of this sharing of your personal information, please visit readerservice.com/consumerschoice or call 1-800-873-8635. **Notice to California Residents**—Under California law, you have specific rights to control and access your data. For more information on these rights and how to exercise them, visit corporate.harlequin.com/california-privacy.

HD21R

Return to Jackson Falls for the next sexy and irresistible book in Synithia Williams's reader-favorite series featuring the Robidoux family!

When everything is working to keep them apart, can these two former enemies learn to trust one another for a chance at forever?

Read on for a sneak peek at
Careless Whispers

She turned to face him, her heart pounding again and a dozen warning bells going off in her head. She should shut down the flirting, but the look in Alex's eyes said he was willing to go with her down this path. "I've got some experience with wanting the wrong man."

"But that's all in your past now." He took a half step closer.

She shook her head. She'd never been good at not going for what she wanted. Her ego needed stroking, and Alex with his quiet understanding and empathy had shown her more care than anyone had in a long time. She'd be smarter this time. This was just to quell her curiosity. People said there was a thin line between love and hate. Maybe all their bickering had just been leading to this.

"Not quite," she said, choosing her next words carefully. She pretended to check the list in her box. "I find myself thinking about someone who I once despised. I miss clashing with him daily. I enjoy the verbal sparring. Not to mention he recently wrapped his arms around me, and for some reason I can't get that out of my head." She glanced at him. "He's stronger than I imagined. His embrace comforting in a way I didn't realize I'd like. It makes me want more even though I know I shouldn't."

Alex stilled next to her. "What are you going to do about this ill-advised craving?"

"It kind of depends on him," she said. "I think he's interested, but I can't be sure. And you know I can never offer myself to a man who didn't want me." She said the last part with a slight shrug. Though her heart imitated a hummingbird flitting against her ribs, and a mixture of excitement and adrenaline flowed with each beat.

Alex slid closer, closing the distance between them and filling her senses with him. He pulled the paper out of her hands. "What if he wants you, too?"

His deep voice slid over her like warm satin. She faced him and met his dark eyes. "Then I'm in trouble, because I'm no good at saying no to the things I want but shouldn't have."

Don't miss what happens next in...
Careless Whispers *by Synithia Williams.*

Available March 2021 wherever
HQN books and ebooks are sold.

HQNBooks.com